BLACK
BUTTERFLIES

BLACK
BUTTERFLIES

Short Contemporary Fictions

Chase Maxwell

For

"Jazz," my butterfly

"When hell rains on you, sometimes you just have to blow the torch back"

CONTENTS

BLACK

ROSE

BLACK ROSE

"They said I wasn't built like that,

until I squeezed the hammer.

Shots fired! Shots fired!

What had I done, killing my own? Now what?

Chase Maxwell

The last time they recalled being happy as *one* was that time in St. Thomas, the night of the all-white party. They were well-off then, climbing the top of the world. Friendships have been wrecked. Bonds between brothers have withered like molten steel, like dried up black rose leaves. Everything is lost, almost. Each has few breaths left. How many times does a man's heart have to be broken to start a war? It depends on the bow that breaks it; especially if it is an arrow of betrayal. Six bullets narrowly decimated the heart friendship claimed to love. Who would have thought the mighty ring would fall. Oh my! How things have changed. They should've seen it coming, even before frantic hips touched.

There was something about the way the day started—Romeo knew things were going to be bad. Too many guns, too many women, too much trouble he'd had with the law and the Black Rose Firm. Even his wife is baffled, he's still alive. Romeo has had enough of that life. It's hard to quit what claims to own your next breath. The only way out is in a casket. "Strap up and let's do this," says his wife. Yet in a world of violence and corruption, there are things more lethal than looking down the barrel of a gun.

"I'm about to make baby girl sing tonight," Romeo, slouched on the couch, carefully slips his Glock pistol in the holster behind his back.

"Who or what are you talking about, the gun or Jazz?" Emilio, Romeo's twin brother asks.

"Both," Romeo replies with a huge grin.

"I don't know. I heard she runs things," Orlando, their little brother chimes in, struggling not to ruin his pretty boy face on the floor, after more than six dozen push-ups.

"You've been away too long," Romeo laughs. "The trick is, you let them think they do," he brags, offering his little brother a hand to help him up.

Emilio peeks out the window and tightens his face with a reluctant smile. Jazz walks in.

"Hey, love. *Sak pase?* (What's up?)" she sits on her husband's lap.

"What's going on, boo?" Romeo says to her.

Jazz plants a long kiss on his lips.

"Now, what was it you were saying about running things?" she squeezes Romeo's face against her chest.

"You like that, don't you?" she mocks him.

The other two Blaise brothers are laughing to themselves, amused by Romeo's pretentious swagger, shaking their heads.

"See? I told you," Emilio tells Orlando.

"That's right, big sis, he better put some respect on your name," Orlando edges out with a piercing laughter.

Suddenly, shots ring out from outside the living room window. A cloud of smoke erupts. "I'm hit, I'm hit," Romeo's body jerks like a wounded stag. By the time Emilio and Orlando make it out to the front porch, their guns drawn, a black truck speedily turns the corner up the block; its tires screeching past the loud chatter of terrified neighbors running for cover.

———

What could be worse than staring down the barrel of a gun? Seeing the woman you love nearly get wiped away by stray bullets intended for your own flesh.

"We got to end this. There is too much going on. We must end this war. I can't take another day like this," Jazz cries out. Though unscathed, the never-ending presence of danger crawls on her skin, enough to drive a soul to jump off a cliff.

"Thank God, Romeo is going to be all right," Emilio sighs at the hospital, raising both hands to his face. The doctors say it was only a few grazed bullets, but this is the second time in less than six months someone has attempted to end Romeo's life. The failed assassination has far more to do with love, however twisted, than simply a random hit of a life of crime. Jazz knows what it will take to end the war. A slew of rash feats by her husband has turned old friends into foes. She now finds herself in the middle of the tug of war. What she is asked to sacrifice to save her husband's life will cost her more than she is willing to bear. She's left without a choice. "Strap up," she'd told Romeo; it almost cost her the only man she has ever loved.

The Blaise brothers weren't always bad boys. They grew up in South Side, Jamaica, in Queens, New York. Emilio and his younger brother, Orlando, always got into trouble. Romeo was the quiet one. The twins, Romeo, and Emilio, after graduating from high school, went on to study business administration at a school in Long Island. It was where Romeo proposed to the love of his life and eventually married Jazz before finishing school a year ago.

The Black Rose Firm—the underground money laundering operation began around the same time. Trey, a fellow student at the university, was the mastermind behind it all. Orlando had been serving time in Rikers since he turned eighteen for a gun and assault charge. He once swore, he would take a bullet for Trey. Things weren't what they seemed to be. Orlando is out and is now looking to avenge his unjustifiable imprisonment. "Trey has it coming," he says. They were once part of a band of brotherhood. Trey had been like blood brothers. Betrayal and indiscretions have changed everything.

"I never thought getting involved with the Black Rose Firm would threaten to tear my life apart," Romeo concedes. The Blaise brothers are back at the house, trying to figure out the best way to settle the score with a wicked man who wouldn't mind seeing each one in a casket.

"It's all your fault, Romeo," Orlando leers at his brother. "You couldn't keep your hands off his woman."

"*Alright,* guys. Come on now. What's done is done," Emilio interjects.

Jazz is quiet. She knows it's true. They are all gathered in the basement like caged birds.

"Romeo, is there any way we can pay this guy to get him off our backs?" Emilio proposes.

"Hell no!" Orlando protests. "Trey set me up, and now he's got to pay."

Romeo scours the room and finally lands eye to eye with his wife.

"You *alright,* babe?" he asks.

Jazz nods. Her face tells him everything he's afraid to hear.

"Look at us?" he says. "We're all crowded in a dark basement like wild animals. Something has to give. Trey doesn't want my money."

"If he wants our blood, I want his blood," Orlando rages.

"*Man,* shut up already," Emilio yells at him.

"What? What are you going to do?" Orlando pulls out his gun.

"I wish you would," Emilio stares him down with a snicker.

"You've gotten soft!" Orlando shouts, flipping the gun around with his index finger.

"You're right. I've gotten smarter, because *that* right here is stupid," Emilio grabs the gun from him.

"How do I get myself out of this mess?" Romeo thinks to himself. It all started when a "happy hour" of what was far from a binge drinking feast in his office led to him savoring a forbidden fruit. Romeo wishes he could take it back. It is the ultimate sin to filch another man's grape or poke his jar of honey. It was the only rule of the game. "What's stolen in secret will haunt you until the day you die," Trey warned Romeo.

The next morning, Jazz is missing. The Blaise brothers are on their way to Jermaine's house. He's like a Black Rose Firm underboss. Romeo and his brothers have been looking everywhere for Jazz. Jermaine still considers them family. Yet the brothers strap their guns as though expecting war. They can't trust no one. Emilio goes in first. They must exercise caution. This part of *Bed-Stuy* in Brooklyn isn't what it used to be. Any suspicious activities, the cops now show up in a flash. Orlando is excessively hot-tempered. He'll want to start a riot. It's best that he stays in the car. Romeo can't keep it together. His wife is missing. He thinks something horrible has happened to Jazz. He's panicky, holding a Glock on his lap. Romeo worries, Jazz's sudden disappearance may have something to do with the text messages Trey sent her, and the fancy jewelries she had received from him. Orlando, as well, is edgy behind the wheel. "Another thirty seconds Emilio doesn't come out, I'm going in," he tells Romeo.

Sneaking out the house, Jazz headed straight to barred territory. As she makes her way through the gate, her heart is racing. She's tense but not afraid. As soon as she gets to the door, "You know, showing up like this, you have enough...forget it; you're a woman," Trey tells her. "Having said that, I'm glad you're here," he offers Jazz something to drink after letting her in and ordering his heavily armed security staff to leave the living room.

"No, thank you," Jazz politely declines.

Trey takes off his shirt, showing off his husky chest. He's tall, dark, and handsome. It is, however, the last thing on Jazz's mind. Trey ushers her to a seat.

"So, what can I do for you, beautiful?" He takes a seat across from Jazz, laughing hysterically.

"It's such a shame that a wicked man like you has that kind of smile," Jazz sighs and lifts her brows.

"Please, continue to charm me. It makes me want you even more," Trey edges out with a callous grin.

"Let's cut through the bull," Jazz says. "You almost killed my husband, and I could've been dead as well."

Trey gnashes his teeth. "First of all, I have no idea what you're talking about. And if I did hire someone to kill him, they would know better not to hurt you," he stands up and starts pacing the room.

"That bastard almost killed us all, Trey. I want my life back," Jazz pleads with him. She follows Trey and stands in his path. Jazz runs her hands on his chest. They're like rose petals brushing against dark steel. "We were once family," she says.

"Well, that was before your husband slept with my woman," Trey stares at her, coldly. Yet his heart is warm. "What if I had done the same thing!" he shouts, slowly letting out a gust of angry breaths.

"Is that what this is about? Is it me you really want, Trey?" Jazz takes her clothes off. "Well, here I am. Do what you will with me. We want out, Trey. I want out," she stands before him with gaping eyes and her flesh bare.

Trey catches a whiff of her winded perfume. She smells like chocolate infused in freshly squeezed orange. Jazz's hips, lusciously curved. Her skin, smooth and glistening. Trey wants her. He always has. But not like this. He's angry, full of lust, but his pride craves more than the ardent flavor of the brown skinned flesh he longed for since freshman year in high school. Wildly aroused, *should I?* He does. Trey grabs hold of Jazz, turns her, forcefully hurling her hands against the wall. He holds her waist—rage in his thrusts—while remorse fills his heart.

At Jermaine's house, Romeo and Orlando still waiting for Emilio to come out, a car pulls up behind their rental burgundy truck. It's a black sedan, with the emblem "BR" inscribed in white gold on its front grill—undoubtedly part of the Black Rose fleet.

"Oh fuck," Orlando ducks behind the wheel.

"No way," Romeo yells out. He notices Jazz coming out of the black sedan, Trey trailing behind. Romeo steps out. Without a word, he points his gun sideways at Trey. The driver of the sedan, and the woman next to him, both Black Rose security deputies, quickly exit the vehicle and brandish their weapons. Their gun barrels aiming static at Romeo.

"It's okay, Romeo. The war is over now," Jazz, tears in her eyes, tells her husband.

Romeo, angry and confused. "What are you talking about, Jazz? We can't trust this guy," Romeo shouts, still holding the gun.

"I've handled it, baby. We're good now," Jazz tells him, her body shaking.

"What did you do? What did you do, Jazz?" Romeo yells at her, his eyes raining tears.

Jazz puts her head down.

"Now you know what it feels like," Trey rants out with a smirk.

Orlando runs out the car, pointing his gun towards Trey. They hear police sirens, not too far away. Emilio at that moment is coming out of the apartment. The woman holding the gun, one of the remnants and faithful Black Rose deputy, starts to fire at him. A hail of gunfire follows.

Minutes later, "We got seven bodies down," one of the officers yells out.

"Are you related to any of them?" another officer probes Jermaine, who quickly ran outside after hearing gunfire.

"Yeah, we're all family," he says, in utter shock.

"It's been a while since I've seen anything like this. What the heck happened here?" the officer asks.

"Love betrayed can make you do some weird things," Jermaine says, inhaling a long whiff of air.

SHAI'S

PARADISE

SHAI'S PARADISE

THE ONE

I have often wondered why she looks at me this way—her eyes seemingly dimming with lust. Tonight, her gaze is fraught with cynicism.

"Max!"

I ignore her shout.

"So, tell me, how was New York?"

She sulks when I don't answer. I like a woman with her temperament. I love who she is—hot-blooded, her heart full of charisma. Her wrath throttles over the sheets like a rowing fantasy ride. Her love is like magic. Who knows such a woman? She's all mine. Not today. Perhaps not ever, if she finds out what I have done.

"If you're not going to tell me how your trip was, you won't ever touch me again," she says.

That is usually my punishment. How do you tell a woman like that about your sins? How can you? Her skin is now rubbing against mine. Her lips canvasing my bare chest. No doubt, she wants to get it out of me.

"Everything went well," I tell her.

Like a bee craving for honey, I pursue her front with swiftness. Whirling, as if in between the wings of a butterfly, my head sails past the banks of her crust.

"Max, I love you," she whimpers, firmly gripping my hands. I sink deeper into the abyss.

Downtown Atlanta

"So Max, how was the plane ride back home?" Stephan asks.

"I don't feel well today," I say to him. We've been friends for a long time. Yet I'm terribly afraid to utter anything. "Well, you know," I reluctantly mutter, before admitting it was a fun trip.

He laughs, of course. Stephan knows what's going on. He and I have been going through this since high school. He taps his pen on the desk, gawking at me.

"Max, you have to stop this," he says.

Only if it were that easy, I'm thinking.

"Gosh! The woman has given you everything," he growls once more.

I surely don't want anything else from Shai. She's a good woman. I can't seem to figure out why we men cheat. Perhaps we never have enough. There are things second nature to some men. Some women, as well, I suppose. It's not a sickness in me. It feels part of who I'm expected to be. As if Stephan read my mind, "I gather that's why you will never get married," he quips. Holy matrimony will never be for me, I tell him. Not until I'm cured.

"Of what?"

"Let me make this clear. I don't intently go out pursuing other women. Sometimes—"

"Ain't no sometimes," Stephan interrupts. "Keep it in your pants or it's not going to end well for you."

"I wouldn't necessarily call it an abysmal disease. But I can't help loving too much the scent of a woman," I tell Stephan.

I can't remember the last time I've set my foot inside a church. Still, I feel like I'm committing a sin. There are times, I ask myself, why was a woman created? She's both a blessing and a curse. Her beauty is my torment. Her touch, my joy; I hope her scorn doesn't send me to *Hell*.

It's three o'clock in the afternoon, almost time for me to return home. My cell phone has been vibrating all day. I received a couple of text messages from the love of my life. Shai and I normally speak every day when I'm at work. Today, I'm tired. Perhaps exhausted from guilt.

"Mr. Bane, someone's in the lobby asking for you," one of the interns blurts out with a smirk. There aren't ever any secrets with so many snooping ears at the office.

"Do you know who it is?" I ask. She doesn't even bother to answer. My indiscretions have been paraded like unsavory flicks at a movie theater. Something terrible happened on my last trip. I can't tell Stephan about it. I get to the lobby, it's not who I expected it to be. It is my worst nightmare. She has followed me home. "

"What are you doing here, Kelly?" I am fuming; a scorching thrust inside my ribs. Nonetheless, I'm afraid to show it.

"What, you're not happy to see your woman, Max?"

She has a conniving frown on her face. Taking her by the hands, I pull her away. We walk to the corner near the coffee shop. This round face guy is so lost in her; he either does not care or is oblivious to the fact that I'm standing there. I can't blame him. I see what he sees—an exceptionally beautiful woman. Yet today is not the day to immerse in Kelly's beauty. Why is she wearing a sheer lace dress in the middle of the day in Atlanta? Her curves are exposed, undoubtedly to provoke me. Or maybe she realizes this is how I can be tamed.

Kelly claims, she has been in town for a couple of days. So why suddenly is she here without warning?

"Kelly, listen, honey—you need to go home."

"So narcissistic of you, Max. You were the one begging not to leave the other night," She starts laughing.

We order two cups of cappuccino from the coffee shop.

"I wish I was here for you, but Mario called," Kelly says, arching slightly over her cup.

"Sweetheart, I don't care if you're here for me, or for whomever. You can't just show up like this," I tell her.

She leans back and takes out her lipstick from her purse to polish her lips.

"Okay, Max. I'm leaving."

She must think her seductive play leaves me unimpressed. It is igniting a searing rush in me, waiting to be set ablaze. We argue walking over to the next block and cram a seat across the street in the park. More men are staring at her. She finds delight in their uninhibited thirst. Some guy winced at her, she says. If I wasn't at times that way myself, I would have thought all men were callous. I must get back to work, but I'm curious to find out why Kelly showed up unexpectedly.

"I have to get back to work. Why didn't you tell me you were coming?" I ask.

She does not utter a word.

"Kelly, answer me?"

She does nothing but stares at me. As I'm getting up to leave, "Max, find a way to be with me tonight," she says.

Is she kidding me? I have to go home to Shai. "Didn't Mario call, go to him!" I say to her, cringing inward.

Her expression changes. She looks tense, trying to hide a sad face.

I'm regretting every word, yet I can't bring myself to apologize.

"Max," Kelly says. "Don't play dumb. I know you crave what we had last week."

For some reason, I'm feeling as though I had committed adultery. Kelly and I had awakened next to each other many times. The week prior, I apparently aroused what no man should in a woman, if he's not ready to nurture its flames. I don't know what drove me to say it, but I told Kelly I loved her. The problem is, I meant it; and she knows it. She has traveled all the way from New York, to claim something I'm not sure I can freely give. Has anyone ever loved two people at the same time? Even if such a thing can happen, I love Shai too much to hand my heart over to another woman. Stephan often says I'm a fool. He thinks once a man is unfaithful with his flesh, his heart usually follows. I don't agree with him. Yet I find myself entangled in what I thought could never happen to me. I once dated this girl, who struggled not to fall prey to such a tainted love. She claimed it would never happen to us. I ended up being the victim in a love triangle. Perhaps she had always wanted to leave and found a bitter excuse for the quickest exit out of my life. Surely, I was the one she loved less. Perhaps Stephan's assessment of love enticed by lustful temptation is not so skewed after all. My love for Shai had gone unmatched, until meeting Kelly. Undoubtedly, she and I can never have what Shai and I have. Now, I'm not certain of that. I didn't go looking for another love—it found me. Perhaps I did draw in its bait, by bargaining the comfort of a perfect love. Shai is equally stunning. She has the most gorgeous set of eyes I have ever seen on a woman. They have been staunchly admired jewels since she and I met freshman year in college. But this has nothing to do with looks. I think I may have allowed my heart to slip into another woman's arms.

"So, you're coming?" Kelly lifts her voice. I'm already guilt-ridden. I will feel even worse if I decline her invitation. Then again, I have a way out.

"Mario called, you said. Didn't you?" My only defense against this type of attraction. Although perverse, I'm hoping it doesn't push her into the arms of another man.

"I already saw him last night. He asked me to marry him, but it's not what you and I have," Kelly counters.

My mind must really be sick. Part of me is overjoyed she had turned him down. Men, women, we are all selfish when it comes to love. Even a bit ruthless, I'll go so far to add. I gather the heart is. It wants what it wants regardless the cost.

"It's rare to find men like you," Kelly vents. She refers to our lovemaking as animalistic creatures with kind hearts. The kind that turns a lover's bed into a forbidden paradise. We're leaving the park; Kelly wants to reassure me of her firm grip. She holds me close, blowing cool air in my ear. She whispered a wish that shot warmly down my spine. I find a makeshift den, made of arching trees. The perfect landscape for carnal wildfire. Kelly holds on to me and bows like a sacrilegious creature in a garden of love. I grunt, slowly exhaling. "There is no other woman like me," she brags.

I get back to the office to abhorrent sneers. Everyone here loves Shai. They all want me to marry her. Some are brash; they come right out and say it. Others hide their lippy thoughts behind closed doors. I'm foolishly audacious; it's only a matter of time before Shai leaves me, they say. If I'm so arrogant, what are they? Take Richard for instance. He's married and has three children. And yet, every night he goes out to the bar chasing women. He had even dared to make a naughty proposal to my wife. Okay, Shai is not my wife, but I promised to make her my bride one day. I first have to get over this thing, the salacious web I have gotten myself into. Kelly hates being the other woman, referring to herself as a kept woman. It's not fitting for her to think in such way, being that I am not yet a married man. When I told Kelly, she wasn't my mistress, she said it was a puffed up lie. How then can she lay blame on me? Shai and I have been together for over four years. She asked me to move in two years ago. I thought it would've put an end to my shameless escapades. I love Shai. Although now, I'm not sure about a lot of things.

Early evening, Shai and I are close to finishing dinner. I'm speaking as if it isn't me, as though driven by exterior impulse.

"Babe, the boys and I are hanging out tonight." I can't even look at her eyes.

"Oh! Cool. Can I come?"

I love when Shai is around on outings with the guys. She's sometimes the only girl amid loud, obnoxious men, but she can hold her own. Especially when it comes to sports. But not tonight.

"Uh... we're playing pool at Jason's house," I tell her. She hates going to his house.

"That sucks. Maybe next time."

I want to run, but I can't. I'm torn, muddled by love. I leave her with a kiss, but Shai's lips taste bitter.

I get in the car, my heart racing. There's this volcanic excitement, which often gives way to unseemly affairs. I stop by the winery to get a bottle of Chardonnay, Kelly's favorite. It will help calm my nerves. I began to develop this new thirst ever since I met Kelly last year. The lure of her charm caught me by surprise. She's the type of woman who compels men to listen when she talks. I'm hoping that's all we'll do— talk unreservedly about what's gotten our hearts growing weak. The remedy, Stephan says, is not to allow any other woman to get close. Some women have this thing about them. It grabs you, holds you in place, and refuses to let go. Whatever that is, Kelly has it. It's beginning to pull me away from Shai.

I enter the hotel lobby; Kelly is sitting in the lounge flicking her hair. She has on knee-high tan boots, with a white baby doll dress. She's a shade lighter than Shai, Kelly's pale brown skinned, inherited from her French European farther, and her mother, a black woman from New Orleans. Kelly spots me. Her eyes look moist, reddened.

"What's wrong?" I ask.

She uncrosses her legs, revealing curvy thighs, and once again extends one leg over the other.

"I'm making a fool of myself," she says.

I'm not quite sure what she means. But each word entices me to comfort her. Frankly, I'm tempted to do much more. We go up to her room; Kelly starts wallowing in self-pity, calling herself a slut. Her sudden implosion is beyond me. She's like a goddess. I've never thought of her as anything but a prized jewel. Her eyes are glittery. They snare me, holding me captive of their glossy lure. I offer her a glass of wine.

"No, Max. I'm used to men begging to have me. But I'm here chasing after you like a schoolgirl," she sobs.

I wipe her cheek with a kiss. There is this unexplainable allure, watching a woman spew out what's in her heart. It shoots like an arrow into my chest. I can't let my guard down. Love burns when it falls apart. I was about to walk out, after Kelly told me to go back home. But then, something came over me.

"I'm staying. I don't want to leave you here all alone," I say to her.

"Max, please go home," she says, eyeing me with a sorrowful gaze.

Seeing her weeping, she doesn't look like the *other woman.*

"Come here," I call out to her.

Kelly sits on my lap. "I love you," I whisper in her ear, afraid of my own words. Staring into her eyes, I feel her breathing heavily. I trace her jaw line with my lips, blowing onto her neck.

"Max! Please—" her body jerks.

Placing my hand under her dress, she's flushed, a slight beam on her face.

"Max!"

"Shh...Not another word," I tell her.

Her blush hidden behind a stream of tears, I press her against me, cradling her shoulders and moving gently while swaying my hips. More tears flow down her face. It cracks her stubborn mien. Something in me engrosses each thrust as though in haste to surrender.

"Do you really love me, Kelly?"

"Yes, Max."

I muzzle her screams into my lips. This night is unlike any other. I feel condemned, without fear of reprimand.

WHOM

I Can't believe it has happened again. I've opened up my heart to Kelly. A woman knows. She senses when she has broken down a man's wall. Driving home, I'm all confused. I guess part of me wanted to find out if it was true—what was burning in me. When I saw Kelly earlier at work, I tried my best to hide a sin. It is a haunting evil when one's heart is compromised. There is no such a thing as the game of infidelity. It just happens. Rapidly descending into a silo of tormented souls, as soon as I had stepped foot in the lobby, seeing Kelly again, I wanted to strip her clothes off. Even so, it was more than lust. It felt like a blend of eroticism and belonging. I'm well aware of what it feels like—butterflies in my stomach when I'm with Shai. And now, Kelly has done it. She has me soaring with boundless sentiments.

I pull over a block away from the house. *I can't do this to Shai.* She's been there for me through everything. She's been my world. When we met, I had nothing. Shai pushed me to finish school. So here I am today—an accomplished journalist—a black man with his head up. And it's all because of Shai. Even before she and I started dating, she'd always come through. When my mother passed away my junior year in college, distraught and financially insolvent, I had no clue how I was going to pay for the funeral. Raised in public housing without a father, Mom was the only family I had. Shai helped me take out a loan to pay for the funeral. "That's what best friends do," she said.

What is it about Kelly that's gotten me to feel so pigheaded? Perhaps it was selfish arrogance on my part, mocking Stephan's warning. The road to infidelity may start with lust, but if one is not careful, "dammit!" I pound the wheel. I can't leave Shai. I love her just as much. I don't know anymore. I reverse slowly into the driveway, edgy, with a surge of unexplainable rage. I get inside the house, Shai is in bed, sound asleep. She looks like an angel. I lie down next to her, but my arm isn't wrapped around her waist as usual.

Dammit! She's up.

"My baby is home," Shai mumbles to herself, nudging her back closer to me. I'm hoping she will go back to sleep. She grabs me and says, "I miss you. I called but you didn't pick up."

I don't feel right.

"I'm a bit tired," I say to her.

"What! You? Mr. Iron Man!"

I try to offer a swift smile. But whatever she sees is not genuine. I have never denied her love. This time, I did. Something is happening to me.

I wake up on a Saturday morning; breakfast is already on the table. Shai kisses me on my bare back. She's jovial, looking amused as usual. *Does she not realize what happened last night? How naïve can she be? Perhaps she's not. It's just a trap.* Our den of paradise has been infiltrated.

"Did you have fun last night?" she asks.

I always make sure the boys can cover. I'm finally realizing it is not a guiltless burden.

"Max, are you all right? You didn't answer me," Shai's stunning amber, mystical eyes, piercing through me.

"Shai, sit down. I have something to ask you?"

Her face is brimming with curiosity. I feel trapped.

"Are you cheating on me?" I ask.

"What! Me? Cheating?" she takes a sip of her orange juice, frantically shaking her head. "Is that why you didn't want me last night?"

"I'm waiting for an answer," I say to her.

"Oh please, Max. You would know it. Trust me. You would know if I had been with another man."

"So, you're all nine."

"I'm all yours, Max. I've given you all of me, in and out of bed."

There's no doubt, she's laid her soul bare. But how does a heart feeling ensnared justify guilt? Shai wants to know why I'm all of a sudden questioning her loyalty. She's never been a cynic. Sometimes I wish she were. It would free me of my own remorse. I would feel better if she were the one to walk away.

"How do I know what you do when I'm away," I tell her.

Shai frowns, biting her lips, and then let out a cold grin. "Just like I don't know what you do when you're away," she says.

———

Today is CJ's wedding. He's an old college roommate. It was a relief he didn't ask me to be his best man. It would've had me too close to the altar of holy matrimony. Shai is throwing up again. She's feeling nauseous all the time. Of all days, why pick this day to tell me about her ailing stomach. She desperately wants to have a child. It hasn't happened yet. I'm kind of hoping baby luck waits until after we get married.

"And when will that be?" Shai often asks. She thinks waiting until we tie the knot is such a silly idea. I guess if a baby comes first, then I'll have no choice but to marry her. Time waits on no one, Shai says. Why rush into marriage? My heart will forever be hers. That was before I met Kelly.

"Shai, come on! We're going to miss the wedding ceremony."

She finally comes out of the bathroom. Her face, the color of ash.

"What's the matter, love?" I ask.

"Nothing. We're not pregnant. It should make you feel better," she pounces, her voice ruffled.

"No worries, okay? We'll just have to go back to the doctor," I cradle her in my arms and dash her lips with a kiss.

We are sure to miss the ceremonious vows at the church; so, we head straight to the banquet hall. We get there, everything looks immaculate and white, even the marble floor. It might as well be a place of worship. I'm feeling the sting of remorse.

"Greetings! And good afternoon, lovebirds," this cheerful looking guy greets us. "You're a bit early; and if I didn't already meet them, I would've thought you guys were the bride and groom," he remarks with an awkward laugh.

The hotel attendant has us take a seat in the front lounge. We'll get to see CJ and his bride upon arrival. We wait for what seems like hours. Shai looks amazing in her closefitting white satin gown. "You are an incredibly splendid looking woman," I say to her, as the wedding party comes in.

"Hey Max, good to see you," CJ taps me on the shoulder. "You're still a fine-looking black woman," he says to Shai, patting her cheek.

"Congratulations, CJ. Best of luck to you guys," she tells him.

Shai smiles, but I know deep down she wishes it was the other way around. CJ and his bride, Vanessa, had been dating since senior year in college. They have finally tied the knot after five years. CJ once said, living apart made him and Vanessa appreciate each other more. I wonder how long they will last, living under the same roof.

"They look so happy, don't they?" Shai chimes in. All she has gotten from me is a measly engagement ring, which she says doesn't mean crap. I have had enough of the wedding festivity. I love what it epitomizes. I want it for me and Shai. Then again, I can't help but to think about Kelly. Ditching the party early, we get in the car, I'm feeling light-headed from two vodka glasses.

"I love you, Max. But waiting really hurts my pride," is the first thing Shai shells out.

Speechless and woozy behind the wheel, I ask Shai to drive. I'm beginning to think, if we do get married, it will make everything go away. What if it doesn't? Then I'm stuck holding the knife of betrayal in our marriage. I've asked some of the women at the office what would they do if they were in my shoes? Men, like me, are nothing but spineless scoundrels, they heckled. Most men would not admit it. Even married men, I suppose. But some women are "kryptonite." They whisk you into submission. Don't get too close to a woman, Mom would say. If she wants you, she'll make your heart bleed. The draw of a woman is as powerful as narcotics, she said. Mom once told me a story about a young woman, whose feminine allure so intoxicating, it persuaded a king to surrender half of his kingdom, just so he could watch her twirling.

In a couple of weeks, it's Kelly's birthday. She wants me to come to New York. I have to find a way. I shouldn't feel so thrilled about visiting her. But I am. I tell Shai, I have to meet with a publisher in New Yok. She knows how much it means, finally realizing my dream of getting my book published. I had helped a subsidiary of the renowned publishing house with an article about a celebrity. I'm owed a favor. Shai wants to come along this time. Why bother? I say to her. We would only be in New York for no more than two days. I suggest planning a trip to the Big Apple the following month. We can then stay a whole week. We'll have more time to enjoy the city. She agrees. "Max, you're always thoughtful," she smashes my lips with a kiss. I feel like a jerk, an effeminate coward. Just as I was about to walk away, "Time waits on no one, Max," Shai says. My soul feels uncovered. Bitterly, I press my lips against hers. Slanting her head back, I land a few kisses on her neck. "That, you do well. I need more," she says, removing my hand cuddling her chest.

Two weeks later

I board the plane with unchaste excitement. I love it here in Atlanta, but New York is my second home. It was where the fireworks began, between me and Kelly. She was one of the editors I met with on one of my previous visits with the publishing house. The moment I entered her office, stardust filled the air. We both tried to mask our attraction toward each other. Kelly looked self-assured, undeniably the "straightforward" woman her assistant warned. And yet, I sensed warmness behind Kelly's resilient posture. We sat next to each other to chat. Suddenly, my ribs quivered, inhaling her sweet perfume. Part of me stiffened, the moment intense and maddening all at once. I had never experienced anything like it. Her fragrance, strawberry flavored, enticed me to imagine us in all sorts of places. The following day, Kelly and I met late evening in her office. Meeting with another editor regarding my source for a *Tell All* book allowed me to see Kelly again. Going over some of the edits in my manuscript, out of nowhere, this thing happened. We got into a heated debate about her cutting off a section. Kelly thought it was too obscene. She rattled my nerves. Infuriated, I told her, "You act as though it is unnatural for a woman to sit on a penis. I wish I could demonstrate bringing a woman to climax in such way."

Kelly laughed. "I did not say it was unnatural. For our list, this may be too edgy," she said.

"You suits have no idea how it works in the real world," I told her. "Kelly, just imagine this parallel universe, this space of lost inhibitions, where a man and a woman give in to urges. Do you know how powerful that is? How free the mind becomes?"

"I will not insult you by saying that this work reads like a fan fiction, but it's pretty close."

"All I'm saying is, when I wrote this, it was purely based on an imaginary world. But I know it can happen because of the way I'm feeling right now."

Kelly fidgeted in her seat. "How exactly are you feeling?"

Her perfume running through me and feeling heavy, "I'm hoping this isn't too forward. But I'm attracted to you. I know to have restraint because I'm not one to prey on women. But yes, I think you're hot and have imagined—"

Kelly stared fixedly into my eyes as I spoke. Thinking I might have overstepped professional boundaries, I offer an apology. "I'm sorry. It's getting late. There's hardly anyone left in the building, so I think it's time for me to leave."

"Max, I'm a skilled Brazilian jiu-jitsu. I can handle myself," Kelly said. "It's obvious that you're considerate, in addition to being so good-looking. Since we're being transparent, your story charmed me to the point of feeling warm between my legs."

Then, as though a surge of uncontainable lust entered both of us, Kelly and I rushed toward each other; shoving aside books and a notebook. Kelly's back pasted to her desk, I got on my knees, a dew of honey on my lips. I then got up without a word, walked outside, and hailed a cab back to the hotel. Later that night, Kelly stood outside my hotel room, unannounced.

I GET TO THE AIRPORT AT JFK, Kelly's standing there; looking even more irresistible than the last time I saw her. Her body-hugging, pencil cut skirt snugs her hips like a figurine ornamental. She greets me with a bouquet of roses.

"What kind of woman does this?" I bow to kiss her. "You're making this a difficult choice."

She tugs at my belt buckle. "I'm the type of woman that knows what she wants and how to get it," Kelly responds with a commending grip around my waist. We get in her car, driving to the Upper East Side of Manhattan. This will be my first time visiting her home, since Kelly and I usually meet at this hotel in the city. She's well-off. Kelly is from what many would call "Old money." Her family hails from a generation of well-to-do French entrepreneurs. Still in her thirties, she holds two masters and a law degree from Harvard. But she doesn't practice law nor cares too much about her parents' wealth. She's a free spirit who loves a good story. Although now an editor, Kelly has published a best-selling romance novel. She's humble as apple pie. And yet, at times, I wonder if she's hiding who she really is. She plays shy, but then turns vampish. Pleasant at first glance, Kelly is frosty if she doesn't get her way.

We park at the garage entrance below a high-rise building. "We're here, this is my secret castle," Kelly hands her keys to the valet attendant.

"Good afternoon, Mrs. Kent. Back so soon," he says to her.

Mrs. Kent? I've known Kelly close to a year; her name has always been Alexandre.

"Just get the damn keys," she shrewdly interrupts, as the attendant attempts to greet me. Short and chubby, he dips his head in apparent embarrassment. Kelly either doesn't notice or does not at all care.

"Don't you think you were a little rude," I say to her. "And why does he call you Mrs. Kent?"

"Max, please. This is not the time."

As Kelly is about to plant a kiss on my lips. "Sir, can I help with your luggage," another attendant asks.

"Don't bother, Henry. He's not that type," Kelly tells him.

He stares at me with a puzzling grin. I'm thinking, *oh yeah*, there is a lot about this woman I don't yet know. At this point, I'm not quite sure if I want to find out. Part of me wants to run. But Kelly already has me on a hook. She lives in a majestic condo apartment. The type Shai and I hope to move into one day. Though many journalism awards have been bestowed to me, my paycheck still can't afford a decent home. I've been around people with wealth most of my career as a journalist. With Kelly, I can smell opulence. Perhaps it's from being up-close. Nothing about Kelly is anticlimactic. She's acting snobbish. Not unlike her usual ways when angry.

"So, who are you really, Mrs. Kent?" I ask going up the elevator.

"Wait till we get inside, will you?" Kelly snaps. I'm not comfortable with that answer. I ask yet again, walking to her apartment. She doesn't answer. There's nothing extraordinary inside her condo. Nothing to suggest, she's a wealthy woman. Except, everything looks pristine and white. The view above the city snatches your breath, looking out the towering living room window.

"Hey, Patricia. This is Max," Kelly says to the young lady sitting on the couch.

"Humph! Tall, dark and handsome, just how I like them," Patricia shouts.

"Well, hello to you too," I reply.

She looks to be in her early twenties. As she gets up to shake my hand, she's wearing nothing but silk undergarments. Patricia quickly picks up the sheet on the couch to cover. Kelly doesn't look amused. "We have company; go put some clothes on," she tells Patricia. The young woman ignores her.

"Come with me," Kelly commands. For a moment, I didn't think she was talking to me.

"She's my sister, in case you're wondering," Kelly says, headed toward her bedroom.

"How is that?"

After it had come out, I realized it might have been a stupid question. I'm curious, nonetheless. The young woman looks nothing like her.

"In case I forgot to tell you, my father is now married to a Nigerian woman," Kelly tells me.

Baffled, there's a lot she hasn't been telling me.

"The valet guy calling you, Mrs. *Bent*. What is that about?"

She has other things in mind. Kelly's on her hands and knees. Her bottom facing me.

47

"Must I get undressed? And, it's Kent not Bent," she says.

Edgy, still dumbfounded, and feeling as though the earth is rising under me.

"Kelly...uh..." I try to speak, but I can't.

"C'mon, Max. Please, enough talking."

We touch, as if it is our first time. And do it all over again. The ground, once more, violently propels its strength. There's something sinister about engaging in sensuality, the city skylight scrutinizing you, bare.

"I will never have enough of you," Kelly gasps.

"*Préviens-moi la prochaine fois*," Patricia yells out behind the bedroom door.

"What was that?" I ask.

"Ignore her, she's just jealous," Kelly scoffs.

I'm feeling embarrassed, unable to muffle exhilaration.

"Okay, Kelly," I lay next to her. "No more secrets. We need to talk."

"There's no need for you to get upset, Max. I had just gotten divorced when we met."

I feel like a piece of trash, lying next to her.

"Max, please understand," Kelly kneels on top of me. Her piercing, winsome blue eyes, staring me down. "I was a broken woman, Max. After what you did to me in that office, I became a woman again," Kelly traces her hair back and thrusts her palms against my chest.

"Frankly, Kelly. I think we're—"

I was about to tell her, perhaps we're moving too fast.

"Please, let me finish!" Kelly interjects. "When you said that you had fallen in love with me, Max, I hadn't heard that for so long. Not only had I felt what it's like to be a woman, I became one who could love again."

Kelly says, she's been living in her condo even before her divorce. So everyone still refers to her as Mrs. Kent. The apartment has been a sanctuary ever since she and her ex-husband first separated.

"You just don't know how much I despise that man, Max. That bastard cheated on me with so many different women."

I'm feeling worse than a convict.

Later, "*C'etait bon*?" Patricia says to Kelly. We're in the kitchen preparing dinner. I may not have spoken much French of late, but I understand *bon*.

"What's it to you if it was good," I reply.

Kelly starts laughing. But Patricia only offers a slight giggle. She has a poignant question.

"Max, who were you talking to in the bathroom earlier, whispering?"

Kelly nudges her on the shoulder and tells Patricia to be quiet. Kelly's face narrowing with discomfort.

"Wait, are you married? Is he married, Kelly?" Patricia's voice soars.

She irks me.

"I'm not married," I calmly say to her.

"I heard you calling somebody—baby—and cannot wait to return home," she says.

"Okay, Patricia. That's enough!" Kelly shouts.

Patricia bangs a knife on the counter, almost cutting her finger. "I've lost my appetite; I'm not eating. *Les hommes sont des chiens.*"

I'm peeved and surely do not need all the aggravation. Patricia mutters a few other words in French, which I sense irritates Kelly further. Looking flustered, and moving restlessly around the kitchen, "I think we should eat out," Kelly says.

We're out dining at a Lower East side café, Kelly is not saying much. She claims, she's not angry. But her eyes betray her cover. They gape with repugnance.

"You're gorgeous, Kelly."

"I'm certain, I am not the only woman you charm with these words."

"Is it immoral for me to fall in love?"

"I would lash out my errant thoughts, but it's best to remain silent," Kelly says.

"Walk away then, Kelly. I would chase you around the world."

"You're an expert at melting a woman's heart, Max."

"I'm skillful at a lot of things, to use your own words."

"Stop it, Max," her lips quivering, no doubt hiding an inward smile.

What is it about this woman? Once again, wondering to myself. What is it about Kelly that has gotten me spellbound? Surely, she's the type of woman who can turn a man away from his home. I've been in this game for a long time. This is not what's supposed to happen. Some men cheat yet don't necessarily leave home. I'm feeling differently today. Nothing Kelly has, Shai lacks. There is something in her pulling me. Perhaps she's reflective of what's in me—the fear of being left to fend for myself again. Once railroaded by love, how can you trust it will not yet again vanish? I will never care for a woman more than I have with Shai. Kelly is drawing me in like a magnetic rose, drowning in her.

I would ask some of the married guys at work. I would say to them, describe the forbidden woman. At first, most of them looked puzzled. But then, they defined such woman: voluptuous, sassy, with a fiery lust that never burns out. When asked if they would blindly leave their wives for such erotic utopia, most of them objected. Stephan is the youngest guy in the office yet seemingly the wisest. He and I two years apart, at twenty eight, Stephan is the only one without a companion. "How about a woman who can steer your heart away from your wives?" he once asked. There was a confounding silence that followed. The guys were all at a loss for words. *That!* Kelly possesses. *That,* which cannot be explained. The "It" factor. These men never once denied it could not be done. But there is a woman who can. And in my case, her name is Kelly.

MY HEART

Happy birthday, Kelly. There's a lump in my throat, singing, "Happy birthday to you." Her eyes shifting, a droplet of tear runs over her jaded beam. "Good morning, sunshine," I say to her, wiping her tears.

"Thank you for the beautiful serenade, but am I losing this fight?" she asks.

"What fight? What are you talking about, sweetheart?"

I'm in a daze. Though I shouldn't be. Kelly pushes me away. She has encouraged my vain foolishness. Why make me feel as though I lack compassion?

"Come on! Not today, *Kel.* Couples go through these types of ordeals all the time. What will come of us is destined. Let's enjoy the day"

She rolls out of bed and tap dances her naked flesh to get her phone atop the dresser.

"You know, Max, a wise woman once told me it is never a good thing to bed what's not yours," Kelly idly thumps her cell phone, and then jumps back to bed, hovering over me.

"When is your wise woman going back?" I ask.

"Who? Patricia?" She pulls back her cheeks with a slight snicker. "She's only here for the week."

"Kelly, what criteria in a relationship that determines when someone is *ours?*"

"Good question," she pauses. "Faithfulness, I guess."

"Are you saying, once a man or woman is unfaithful, he or she does not belong to either partner?"

"Where is this leading to, Max?"

"I'm not sure, Kelly. There's just so much on my mind."

Today is my last day in New York. My mind is cluttered. I have no idea what's going to happen with me and Shai. Still, "I'm yours and you're mine," I say to Kelly. She lays her bare body flat on top of me.

"Am I, Max?" she gathers her lips. "How can you be mine when I'm sharing you with another woman?" She dangles her eyes, as if staring into my soul.

I swallow the heavy lump in my throat.

"You know, Max. I've been doing a lot of soul searching. Mario called; he's insisting on making me his wife."

Who's this Mario guy? I'm thinking. Is he a figment of her imagination? She talks about him all the time. He's this rich music mogul in Atlanta, she claims. I've never met him. Sometimes, I think she talks about Mario, hoping to persuade a decision between her and Shai. I run my hands along her spine. Up and down, the tips of my fingers threading.

"How much do you love me, Max?" Kelly stoops back, weaving her body far below.

"Damn! I love you," I shout.

"I need a breath of fresh air," Kelly sighs and gets off the bed.

On the way home the following day, I anticipate facing a whole heap of trouble. On the flight back to Atlanta, I crossed paths with Emma; one of Shai's cousins who lives in New York. The law of atonement catches on, as if guided by fate. Emma had seen me with Kelly at the airport. She tried to hide her face. Yet I knew she had seen Kelly's ardent kiss. Coming off the plane, Emma had a look of disgust on her face. I Knew I was doomed. Whoever says news travels like lightening wasn't kidding. I should know better, publicizing what most people wished they could keep private. I arrive home, Shai is in the middle of the living room, sitting on the floor. A row of photo albums with our pictures rests like impaled planks before her. Shai's eyes are moist red, her mascara running.

"Max, do you know what next week is?" she asks, as soon as I walk in.

My silence is heard.

"For years, I've been waiting, waiting for you to come around, Max," she covers her face with her hands. "Hoping for us to get married," she's breaking down before my eyes. I go to hug her.

"Get your filthy paws off of me, you ungrateful bastard."

"Shai, baby. Whatever it is, we can talk about it."

"You disgusting pig," she throws her arm to land a punch. I catch her hand in midair. "Get out! Get your stuff and get out," she yells.

Shai's wound burns. It scorches like wildfire in me. She sensed unease between us even before Emma told her. I've had a few flings here and there, Shai hardly noticed. But a woman's instinct picks up when a man's heart is compromised. Since I had been going to New York, Shai detected a change. She ignored it, thinking it wasn't something she needed to fuss over. She hates herself, she said. She'd waited, and forfeited so much of her time, trusting that our affection for each other would never run dry. Shai called me a heartless monster. I'm not cold-blooded. She said so much worse I don't care to recall. I'll admit to losing myself in Kelly's fiery eyes, the swing in her waist. How much can a man handle before he breaks? Shai cannot fathom what's happened. In many ways, neither can I.

I don't really have a place to stay. I figure, I'll spend a couple of weeks here in Atlanta, then travel to see Kelly. I can't be alone. Shai had gone to see the doctor about conceiving. She wouldn't tell me what Dr. Blanche said. Both Shai and Kelly are in my head. I would love to surprise Kelly and maybe bring Stephan along. He and Patricia seem like a good fit. They both apparently have high moral standings. Besides, Stephan thinks all black women are goddesses. All women are goddesses, I tell him. But from one black man to another, I appreciate his reverence of black women.

Shai calls. She has good news. Dr. Blanche couldn't find anything wrong. Still, she sounds desolate and angry. My mind is warped. I wish for her to be the mother of my child. Telling her such a thing would be insulting. Kelly rarely talks about having children. Her annoyance at arduous demands of motherhood makes me think she doesn't want any. Hearing Shai's voice floods me with guilt. She's hurt and refuses to talk about us. I'm hoping we can one day rekindle our friendship. I care about her. But I miss Kelly. Shai is crying on the phone.

"It seems like you don't want to even fight for me," she says.

I feel irritated. I love Shai. I don't know anymore. I would hate to marry and still think about other women. Kelly loves me unconditionally. Perhaps it's the other way around. I don't think any man's heart is incapable of loving two women at once. Though commitment is about choice.

"I am not as willing to just let go of you, Shai, the way you've pushed me away. I love being around you and think of us, night and day."

"Yet I'll bet you also think about that woman."

I'm speechless.

"Say something, Max. I don't even know why I'm on the phone with you," Shai angrily shouts.

I have to take everything she throws at me. But her words stab. Would she ever trust me if I were to walk away from Kelly? Would I trust myself to stay away?

"I love you," I say to her. All I hear then, is the stillness of the dial. The words simply fluttered out of my mouth.

I move in with Stephan, until I can figure out what to do. In the meantime, I call Kelly and make plans to visit her in New York. I don't tell her. I want it to be a surprise. "Have Patricia call me," I say to her. Stephan has been unlucky in love. Patricia might be his future bride. I thought Kelly would be a lot more ecstatic, telling her that Shai and I were no longer together. Perhaps she feels remorseful about breaking another woman's heart, having herself felt the sting of a broken marriage. She and I got into a heated argument. For as long as we had been a couple, Shai never really pressured me into marriage. At least not the way Kelly brazenly started forcing my hands. She thinks I'm afraid of commitment. She pissed me off for even suggesting such a thing. It's the last thing I wanted to hear from her, after sacrificing a good thing with Shai. I sense Kelly wants me to marry her, the second I land in New York. I told her, I'm not ready for marriage. I was hoping she would understand. But Kelly hung up the phone. "What's the point in us being together," she said.

A few weeks after Shai and I broke up, I run into her and Emma at the grocery store. Unsure of why that is, I'm furious. Thought I shouldn't be. Having spent so much time apart, Shai looks divine—stunning as ever. I try to talk to her, but Emma stops me. "You've done enough damage, please leave her alone," she says. I think Emma is jealous. She wishes she had what Shai and I shared. Emma and her husband divorced after she'd had numerous affairs. It was one of the reasons I told Shai, I would only get married when I'm ready.

Stephan and I are on our way to visit Kelly
and Patricia in New York. Patricia insists on
meeting Stephan at her place in Midtown,
Manhattan. She's performing in a Broadway
show. I was surprised to learn she's an actress.
I told Stephan not to tell her I'll be tagging
along. Kelly hasn't been the same since she
noticed I wasn't too keen about marrying her.
We talk almost every day, but she sounds
unsettled. "I love you," I tell her. Most times,
she doesn't answer. Kelly knows I love her and
will chase her anywhere. Perhaps the goal is to
have me run after her until I submit. Stephan
and I get on the plane, he's beyond excited. He
and Patricia *hit it off* instantly on the phone.
They are so eager to meet, he was ready to get
on the next flight to New York, viewing the
raunchy pictures Patricia sent him. Though
they haven't yet met, already, they both claim to
be in love. I tell Stephan, he should heed his
own advice—don't turn a blind eye to lust.

We land in New York, without even a word,
Stephan and Patricia start to kiss. They're both
acting like children meeting their first crush.
Patricia is *drop dead* gorgeous. She looks like
what many in Atlanta would call —diva. She

shows up in brand elegance clothing, and a Mercedes limousine, strutting a blonde wig and designer jewelry. There is a quandary or perhaps not. Stephan is average looking. He's not a bad looking guy. However, he's goofy, and not necessarily the most impressive dresser. Patricia apparently isn't bothered by his silly antics nor nerdy attire. It scared me at first, wanting Stephan to meet Patricia. But Stephan is smart and has a good heart. Seeing him and Patricia lock lips, I should find a gig as a matchmaker.

"So, Monsieur Maxwell, is my sister aware? I did not know you were coming," Patricia says, sipping on a Champagne glass inside the limousine.

Stephan likes the way the words roll off her tongue. Especially the way she utters my name. It sounds like smooth Jazz. Stephan gazes into her eyes.

"You look even more irresistible in person," he says.

Patricia laughs and holds his face, kissing Stephan. A year shy of her twenty-fifth birthday, her laughter sounds like teenage giggles.

"Okay, we're leaving now," Patricia rushes Stephan out of the Limo. She has a splendid idea. She hands me the keys to Kelly's apartment; once she finds out it's a surprise visit.

"Y'all two lovebirds behave now," I tap both of them on the shoulder.

"Enjoy your stay, Max," Patricia smooches me on the lips.

Wow! Her lips feel soft. What a delight for Stephan. If this is the way women from her part of town bid adieu, men around the world seriously have to think about moving to France. If she were not Kelly's sister, I would have thought she was flirting with me.

I love coming to New York. Throughout the states, there are beautiful women. But here, they come in all shades: Dark and lovely, tropical ebony, spicy blondes and brunettes. Perhaps that's my problem—rapt at the sight of attractive women. I was hoping never to get hooked, until meting Kelly. Stephan sometimes says, men have no morals. Most women think the way men do, I tell him. They're just too afraid to say it. The limo drops me off.

"Hey, Henry. How are you?" I ask the valet guy.

He looks at me funny.

"I remember you. How are you, Mr. Bane? I mean, Mr. Max," he says.

I hate when he calls me that. I wish he would simply call me, Max.

"Henry, like I've told you, call me Max. That's fine with me," I say to him.

Entering the lobby, the attendant at the desk, a stubby looking black guy, has a stern look on his face, his posture irritable. Hard day at work, I figure, aware of that feeling.

"Hey, boss. How is everything?" I say to him.

"Fine, sir," he answers, coldly.

He must think he's being ridiculed. I'm guessing, not too many people call him boss around here.

"I know how it is in this part of the city; I used to work security at a law firm with *big heads*," I quip.

Bad joke. He's not laughing; not even his stoic posture wanes.

"Hey...uh...Is Mrs. Kent expecting you?" he asks.

"Don't worry about it. I have keys," I tell him.

He frowns, picks up the phone, and starts speaking in what I'm assuming is his native language. He sounds like his arguing. He must really be having a bad day.

"Max!" Henry, running behind me, calls out as I'm getting inside the elevator.

"Later. I'll be back," I shout as the elevator doors close. My mind could have easily deceived me. I swear, I heard him say a curse word. Maybe it was 'Ay Dios Mio.' It's been a long day.

I get upstairs and take out the stem of rose buried underneath my jacket. Its flowery crown has withered. I'll tell Kelly that is how my heart melts for her. She enjoys laughing at my vain remarks.

"Hey, gorgeous!"

She's not answering, but her phone is ringing nonstop. I hear a noise coming from her bedroom. It sounds like...*no way*... I'm not sure. Almost sounds like somebody pounding on a mattress. Kelly's shouts are piercing my ears. I open the door.

"What the fuck!" This huge guy, kneeling behind Kelly, shouts.

"Oh... MAX!" Kelly screams. She's sweaty and looks out of breath.

The guy rolls off the bed, stumbling to get something out of his pants.

"Who the heck is this guy?" he pulls a gun, breathing heavily.

"Oh my goodness, Mario! Don't hurt him. This is Max," Kelly quickly spews out.

The husky, tan skin fella, gasping, and struggling to compose himself, continues to point the gun at me. He's tall, well-built, Spanish looking.

"What is this guy doing here? I thought you said he lives in Atlanta," he barks at Kelly.

"Oh my goodness. I'm so embarrassed. Max, what are you doing here?" Kelly hurries to put on a shirt.

"*Alright.* You need to get out and wait for us until we sort this thing out," Mario says. I guess he really exists.

"Don't worry about me. I'm leaving," I say to him.

Kelly starts crying. She covers her face with a pillow, as if she's about to catch her last breath. "Oh my God, I can't believe this," she muffles her cries, fretfully clutching the pillow.

I grab my luggage and head downstairs. Feeling sluggish, my legs heavy and my throat dry, I want to disappear, fast. I get off the wrong floor, exiting the elevator. *Lobby.* Finally, I reach the ground floor. I'll catch a cab. No. Perhaps an Uber. But where to?

"Mr. Bane, is everything all right?" the guy standing behind the desk hollers.

I wave and walk right out. Henry is standing outside, frantically pacing and staring at his shoes as if in prayer. I'm going to have to walk a few blocks to catch a cab.

"Mr. Max, I don't want to lose my job. Is Ms. Kelly all right?" Henry asks.

I don't want to get him involved. He already thinks he's in enough trouble. I don't even know where I'm going. I'm not angry. Maybe it's just shock.

"You want me to call you a cab?" Henry kindly asks.

I would rather walk. My stomach churning, the summer air is suffocating as if I'm in a coffin. But even buried caskets have bodies. I'm empty.

"Ms. Kelly is a good woman," Henry shouts behind me as I'm leaving.

I make it all the way to 5th Avenue. My phone's been ringing; I don't pick up. It's going to get dark soon. I still have no idea what to do. As deserted as I feel, I want to run back to Kelly. Yet, I know hearing Shai's voice will comfort me. It feels so disgusting of me to call her. It would be wrong to drag Stephan into this. Patricia is Kelly's sister. It would split them, having to choose sides. I look at my phone, Stephan must know. He and Kelly have been the ones shelling my phone with calls. I call Stephan.

"Hello, Max. Where are you?" I can tell, he's freaking out. He and Patricia want to come get me.

Leaning against the entrance rail of the train station, there is loud music in my ear. I think it's coming from a black Mercedes who just pulled up. *Thank God.* It's Stephan and Patricia. Kelly is in the back seat. Stephan and Patricia are quiet. I get in, Kelly is the only one talking.

"Max, I love you. But please understand," her hands are all over me.

I don't even feel them. Call it pride, or whatever, it cripples a man's heart, seeing his woman in such a nauseating position. It feels worse than the slug that could've come out of her lover's gun.

"Oh Max, I felt so unwanted again, after you couldn't decide if you wanted to marry me. And Mario, well—"

I shove her away. "Get your filthy hands off of me."

Stephan starts laughing. Though I know he understands the gravity of my embarrassment, that's just who he is. Patricia joins in the mockery. So furious, I call Kelly a slut. The laughter ends. A brawl ensues in the back. I'm the one at the end of the heavy blows, however. I didn't mean what I said about Kelly. My pride has been stripped of its dignity.

I stay at a hotel. All night, I resist the urge to call Shai. Finally, I muster enough strength to do it.

"Max, what do you want?" her voice stoic and reassured.

We have always been good friends. Then again, it's unfair to lay such a heavy load on her. Shai knows me, nonetheless.

"Max, are you all right?" She asks.

"I miss you, Shai."

"I miss you too, Max. But—" she comes to a sudden halt.

"I want to come home," I say to her. "I need to be home, Shai."

There's an eerie pause. "Max, your home is with that woman."

"I blew it, Shai. I blew it, okay. But I love you," my voice rising.

"Why are you shouting?" she retorts to my visceral plea.

"It's because I miss you. I know that I messed up."

"Max, there's no more fight in me. Sometimes in life, you must learn to live with regrets," she says.

"Shai, Shai!"

I can't believe it. She hangs up. I call her back; she doesn't pick up. I call her again; it goes directly to voicemail.

The next day, Stephan and I are on a plane back to Atlanta. He's boasting about the great night he and Patricia had. I'm so tired listening; I shut him up. "You better watch her; she's got her sister's DNA." It was a bit harsh, yet the only way to stop his annoying swagger.

"Look at you. Have you no shame?" he says. "You've been doing dirt all this time. Now that it's happened to you, you're behaving like a child."

I heard him. But I have other things on my mind.

"I'm going to ask Shai to marry me," I tell Stephan.

He looks amused. As if what I had to say was part of a comedy act.

"I love Shai. I realize now, she's the only one for me."

Stephan doesn't say anything. He simply shakes his head. Then, his expression takes a puzzling turn.

"What's wrong, Stephan?"

His shoulders slump.

"Uh...nothing. Nothing, Max."

The obvious frown on his face prompts me to inquire further.

"I take it, you're not happy with my decision."

After what appears to be a thoughtful gaze, "Max, there's something you need to know," Stephan says.

My heart is pounding. The solemnity in his voice rattles me.

"She's dying," Stephan mutters.

"Dying! Who's dying? Shai? Why the hell would you say that?" I'm waiting for him to tell me it's another one of his sick jokes.

He's not laughing. I spot sorrow on his face. I'm clobbered. My heart hammering with haste.

"Do not play with me, Stephan," I say to him, hoping he will tell me it's a prank. I want to punch him in the face.

"She called me last night," Stephan confesses.

When Shai went back to see Dr. Blanche, she told Shai, imaging results showed an abnormal growth. It is now spreading. I break down crying. "No, not my baby. Not my Shai," slamming the back of the seat in front of me. "I love her, Stephan. I love Shai." My world is ending right before my eyes.

LOST

I get to Atlanta and rush to see Shai from the airport. Shai opens the door, "What do you want?" she asks, standing at the doorway, still in her nightclothes.

"Baby, please. Let me in. Stephan told me."

Her hair is a mess. She looks like someone who hasn't taken good care of herself in years. Still, she looks beautiful. I go into a longwinded speech. She's quiet.

"Shai, did you hear me, dear?"

She lies on the living room floor, staring blindly at the ceiling.

"I have taken you for granted. I've loved you more than any other. You would know it, if not for my foolish impulse leading me astray." I lie on top of her. She's listless, acting as if I'm not even there. "Shai, I would give up my life for yours."

That, she knows is true; no matter the deplorable indiscretion that has betrayed our love. Her eyes are running a bucket of tears.

"Yes, you care about me, Max. But you have savagely ripped my heart apart," she finally speaks.

"Oh dear. My lovely Shai. Please forgive me," I run my fingers through her hair.

"I feel alone, Max. I'm scared. The doctor said, things don't look good. Pretty soon, I may no longer be here."

With both hands, I tensely hold her face. "Stop it, will you? I don't want to hear that."

Her eyes shift to me. "But it's true, Max. Pretty soon, I will no longer be alive. So, get used to it."

Guilt engulfing me, it's getting too much to bear. "Shai, honey. Don't talk like that. I don't want to lose you."

She takes in a few breaths of air. "Are you going to leave now? I've wasted enough of my time on you."

I lean to kiss her. She holds back. "I do not need your sympathy," she says.

———

Six months later

"SWING LOW, SWEET CHARIOT, COMING FOR THE CARRY ME HOME," the choir bellows. It's been six months since Shai and I said our vows while she lay in a hospital bed. Today, our sixth month anniversary, she's being laid to rest. It's been years since I last stepped foot inside a church. Yet on this day, broken, there aren't enough men in the temple to help carry me up the altar. While the choir sang, I prayed for the angels to carry me home to Shai.

"Now, a few words from her husband," the pastor says.

Stephan stands next to me.

"The love of my life is no longer. Her charm may have disappeared into the wind, but her love has not expired. It is still within me. I love you, Shai; I love you with a love I didn't know I had. If only you could see the pain running through me. It burns, Shai. It hurts like current running through my veins." Stephan holds me up.

As they bury my love into the ground, I look up. Kelly is sniffling tears, standing next to her new husband, Mario. Stephan is being comforted by Patricia. I wish, I could join Shai in   paradise.

FROM AFRICA

THERE, WILL COME SOFT RAIN

FROM AFRICA

THERE, WILL COME SOFT RAIN

He seldom sleeps home. In fact, he only comes twice a week. It's been that way ever since we met. Nowadays, he mostly shows his face on Sundays after church. It looks as though he's sneaking to come to us, just as he has each Christmas. I found out, long ago; he doesn't belong to us. His real home is with that woman down the road. That's where he fills up his children's plates. So close, yet so far away is his love. In the middle of that empty road, my son discovered the bastard child. Tears stood in my eyes that day. What's worse, the same day, I found out, I would always be the mistress, never the wife. Who knows who she really is anyway? If she really exists, or perhaps a sad story told just so he wouldn't have to marry me. I guess, I was wrong.

I've shed a lot of tears. I'm still crying. Who the heck cares? The man who once promised me the world?   Surely, not Mr. Fisherman. That's what my son calls him. I told Malcolm, his dad fishes like a prowler of the sea. Destitute women are his prey. His charming bait snares them like vintage wine. I'm no longer a fanatic. There is anger in me. My soul is empty. There is no one there—not even a ghost. I'm not as strong as other single mothers. Even that woman down the road, whom my husband claims to really love, has had enough. Actually, he's *her* husband, but *my man*. No one knows where his shifty hands have now landed. For all he has done, I say, let it   rain.

And Now

"A rainbow of roses"

The plane landed like an angel descending from the clouds. A white, handmade shawl, woven in sphere-shaped pattern covers her buxom frame. "Shamar is here. Oh my goodness, Shamar is here," she sings to herself. He had endured another eighteen-hour flight, which he once swore would be his last.

"Bonjour, my love. Nosy Be welcomes you back," Tabitha greets him with an ardent kiss. He holds on to her; his hands firmly clutching her shoulders. "Oh yes! Shamar, I miss you too," she muffles, feeling the warmth of his kiss on her lips.

"These women still look at you as a charming prince here in Madagascar," Tabitha croons with flattery, seeing so many women staring at Shamar. She and her husband exchange nervous glances. They laugh and occasionally snuggle each other's lips. Shamar strokes Tabitha's hand and cuddles her cheeks. His grip is firm and reassuring. She hasn't been touched like this in years. Neither has her heart been so jubilant. Shamar sits in the passenger seat, relishing the scenic ride home. *What an Adonis god!* Tabitha is thinking to herself. "You are a good-looking man."

"Only good looking?" Shamar laughs. "Well thank you, Tabitha. But you are, as well, a gorgeous woman," he rests his hand above her tights. He hasn't seen Tabitha since after the day they got married. Now he's back to make good on a promise.

"You know, Shamar. I never thought this day would come. I feel alone here," Tabitha scours the hand on her lap. His touch is uplifting. Shamar shoulders the blame for his wife not joining him after all that time.

"I'm here now. Better late than never," he retorts.

Tabitha had done her best not to resent him. But seven years is a long time for a wife to be away from her husband.

"When Mama died, it hurt me that you couldn't come."

Shamar does not answer. How can he? How does a man overcome with guilt comfort his forsaken bride?

"But I'm happy to see you," Tabitha extends her hand to snug her husband's chest.

"Why is it raining so heavily the day I choose to visit?" Shamar asks, trying to change the subject at hand.

"Shamar, my dear. It is because the spirits wish you were here more often."

He clams up. Surely, it is this sort of condemning response he's trying to avoid. "How long before we get there?" he asks.

"See. If you'd come to visit your wife more often, you would have remembered. This is our home, Shamar," Tabitha thumps the car horn. A young lad runs to open the steel gate.

"Home, sweet home," Shamar sighs when he gets inside the house.

"I hope you can find your way around," Tabitha reaches up to kiss him. "You're so tall," she says, hiding her nerves under a soft grin.

As night falls, Shamar lies down next to his wife. Tabitha is a beautiful woman— voluptuous, chocolate skinned, with piercing chestnut brown eyes. Much like her husband's good looks, her beauty is unmatched. Shamar stares at her. He wants her, but he's being coy. Tabitha knows he has a feeble mind, or more so, a resentful spirit.

"In case you're wondering if I have been with another man, no I haven't," she tells Shamar. He feels proud.

"Is it because of my jealous heart?" Shamar shifts his body towards her.

Tabitha knows how bitter he can be. Especially after the fall out they had a few years ago. It nearly ended their marriage.

"And just so you know, I still can find my way around," Shamar puts his hand in between Tabitha's thighs. Her body jerks.

"Be gentle with me," she says, removing her blouse.

"My goodness, Tabitha. You are a divine looking woman," Shamar lets out. He brushes her neck with his lips. She tastes and smells sugared—like perfectly ripe pineapple. "I hope I can at least show you how much I've been thinking about my lovely wife," he gently cups Tabitha's breast. She misses being with him. She craves being touched. Shamar gently nips at every inch of her body. Tabitha resists, feeling herself slipping away.

"It's been a long time," she shells out in submission. Shamar can't get enough of her. He's savoring what he has left behind. He massages Tabitha's breasts, and then covered her nipples with his lips. Now on her back, he runs his lips from neck to waist, at the center line of her spine. Shamar turns Tabitha over, kissing her lips, and then sliding his tongue in a circular motion between her breasts, down to her belly button. Taking his time, he traces his lips back to her neck and under her breasts. It's scorching hot, as their bodies collide under the pungent darkness. Tabitha's shouts, so loud, she wakes up the following day to the sneer of the town villagers.

There is really no one to say goodbye to. No one left behind who will bring down the heart. Tabitha doesn't have any friends. The only family she had was her mother, who died of a broken heart. At least, that's what most believed in the village that raised Tabitha. Josephine, Tabitha's mother, was distraught over Shamar taking so long to come for her daughter. When Shamar accused Tabitha of sleeping with another man, Josephine became even more disheartened. She was beyond angry that Shamar had shamed her family with baseless accusation. Needless to say, the people in the village chastised Tabitha, thinking she had committed adultery. Her husband has now come home to make amends. So he tells Tabitha. He has come to bring her to America.

Death Mountain, Madagascar

Tabitha blesses the ground. She cries over the land, soon she will no longer call home. She wonders if her mother is turning herself in the grave. Although Shamar is a native son, he no longer sees himself as a Malagasy. He, nonetheless, tells his wife, he will forever be one in his heart. His ethnic ways, however, have long vanished. It's no wonder he starts to ridicule Tabitha, when she elects to consult with her mother's spirit.

"What are you doing? The dead know no more than you and I," he scoffs at her. Tabitha doesn't listen to him. She pays homage to her mother against her husband's wishes.

"So, what did dear Mama have to say?" Shamar mocks Tabitha.

It is not good news. She can't risk telling him. She has a lot on her mind—a lot to lose.

"Tell me, Shamar. What have you been doing in the U.S. all that time?" she enquires of her husband.

"What do you mean?" Shamar's careful not to give her an honest answer. He has spent several years without calling. During that time, he hadn't even sent Tabitha a postcard. He undoubtedly can't tell her everything. He had turned hearsay into facts. It was a clever way to cover his own sin. There's not even a smidgeon of suspicion as to why he's back. Tabitha doesn't think he's a saint, but she believes Shamar truly is back to make things right.

"Shamar, thank you. Thank you for keeping your promise. I cannot wait to go to America," Tabitha praises her husband. Though she won't have much to miss, Tabitha is sad. She has spent all twenty-six years of her life in Nosy Be. The only home she had ever known will be a distant memory. However, she will finally be with her husband. She has forgiven Shamar for making her wait. Shamar tells her, it wasn't only because he had been holding a grudge. He blames the lengthy delay, mostly on U.S. immigration bureaucratic red tape. He soon has to find a way to curb his wife's enthusiasm. As each day rolls on, Shamar's feeling more anxious. He feels condemned by his own wrongdoing. There is only one way out.

It is a sunny day in Nosy Be. Tabitha hears what sounds like the faint, melancholic whistling of a sunbird. She's both joyful and gloomy. "Today, I leave home. I'm happy," she tells her husband. But then, she sits alone out in the patio overlooking the colorful village cottages. "Today, I leave you behind, Mother. But I will one day be back," Tabitha gets on her knees and plants her lips on the ground. The crushed stone gravel floor is damp with her tears.

"Come, love. Come! We can't miss the flight," Shamar tells Tabitha.

The airport is only a short ride away. But they must get there early to avoid long lines. Tabitha's face is still wet with tears.

"Get a hold of yourself, woman. Isn't it what you've wanted?" Shamar tries to comfort her.

He and Tabitha get into the taxicab, which had been patiently waiting outside.

"Bonjour, Tabitha," the driver greets her.

"Oh! You know my name?" Tabitha blurts out with an inquiring gaze. It is her first time seeing him.

"Of course, I know your name," he tells her. "Your husband and I are old friends."

"So you know him, Shamar?" Tabitha offers a faint smile, wiping her face with her shawl.

"Yes, sweetheart. I've known Michael for a long time. We crossed paths again just the other day, and he has offered to drop us off," Shamar replies.

"Well, don't forget us when you guys get to Chicago," the driver belts out with a croaky snicker.

Claiming to know his way around better than most, Michael veers towards a rutted, narrow road. Halfway to the airport, the car careens through an alley, abruptly coming to a stop. A large truck cuts in front of the taxicab. Two masked gunmen get out and tap the taxi window with the tip of their automatic machineguns. Tabitha's eyes gaping with fear, she wants to scream. But Michael and Shamar tell her, it's best to remain calm. One of the gunmen orders them to open the car door and tells them to put their heads down. Tabitha is sitting in the back next to Shamar, feeling her heart gyrating. She's scared, gasping, firmly holding Shamar's hand. Her body shaking, she lets out a loud cry. "One more sound and you're dead," one of the armed men yells at her, holding his weapon to her head. The apparent robbers ransack the car, taking with them Shamar and Tabitha's passports, and then drive away.

Hours later

Tabitha and Shamar are at the police station. She's terrified. She can't believe what has happened. "Today, of all days," she cries, holding on tightly to Shamar. She hardly can remember anything. Everything happened in a flash. She can't even speak. Shamar is angry and sweaty, a bewildered look on his face. He's not saying much. He claims, he as well, is too petrified to recall details of the incident. The police are not able to do much without at least a description of the bandits' getaway vehicle. Michael, as well, is speechless. No one remembers anything. They are all pretty much stunned. They're sent home, dejected and confused. Tabitha will have to get a new passport. Seven years, she'd waited. The day of a new beginning has turned into a nightmarish day.

Tabitha and Shamar return home, people in the village are aghast. Tabitha is relieved that she'd taken Shamar's advice to not sell the house. "Don't you worry, love. Once we get your passport done over, we'll get the hell out of here," Shamar reassures Tabitha. It's not so bad. There is still hope. "Thank God we're alive," Shamar wraps his hands around Tabitha's waist. She's cold, angry, and not so hopeful. There's something else. She has a lot on her mind. Something strange caught her eyes. She doesn't know how to tell her husband. Perhaps she was just seeing things. After all, everything was just a blur. It still is. What if she's wrong? What if she'd imagined things? *What if...?* She's thinking, *No way.*

Later on in the evening, Tabitha is sitting across Shamar at the dinner table. Her face dull; her eyes brim with colorless oddity. It must be her luck, she's thinking. Perhaps there's something about the U.S. the spirits don't want her to see. "I still have the scars of Daddy in my heart," Tabitha recalls when her father left. "He took a part of me with him," she cries to Shamar. She has yet to forget that day. It has been etched in memory like a haunting ghost. Tabitha was only ten years old when her father fled to the U.S. with her twin sister. He never came back. Tabitha's heart had been snatched out of her chest. Her mother loathed the bitter loneliness of losing her daughter. It has been a little over fifteen years; Tabitha still feels the sting of despair. The day her father ran away with her twin sister, there was nothing Tabitha could've done. How could anyone foresee the horror about to break many hearts? Perhaps they should have. Especially after Tabitha's father fought so staunchly to have his wife split the twin sisters. After he and Josephine had gotten divorced, Tabitha's father reckoned it was the best way to keep each parent satisfied. Josephine wasn't so thrilled, forced to choose between her daughters. She wanted custody of both girls.

Crossing the river that night, Tabitha sensed her father was up to no good. He had a wicked look in his eyes—an evil twitch. His tic was like a time bomb. Tabitha had escaped her father's ruse but not her sister. Tabitha ran with anguish in her heart and agony like the wind behind her, hurdling back home. The town villagers wanted to kill Animek, Tabitha's father. By then, it was already too late. He was gone. He and Tabitha's twin sister both vanished without a trace. A flight attendant swore she had seen them on the flight to the U.S.; no one has heard from them since. It left everyone's heart troubled and bitter. Even the spirits of the dead cried. And now, Tabitha is wondering to herself, what has her family done to deserve such misfortune?

"Splitting the rose"

Englewood, Chicago. It's three o'clock in the afternoon; McKayla sits near a window overlooking the street. She taps her feet—once, twice, and does it again. She's restless, dismayed, and mad at the world. A single mom, she thinks life has dealt her a bad hand. She's so exasperated and feels so helpless, perpetual sleep crosses her mind. It's almost time to pick up Malcolm from school. She doesn't feel like it. But she has no choice. That's what a single mother does. What Shamar has done to her is reprehensible. Her heart is torn apart, her life in utter chaos. She has few friends, none that she can really trust. She must remain strong, nonetheless. Who's going to take care of Malcolm? He doesn't have a dad. Actually, he does. But McKayla calls Shamar a "sperm donor."

Malcolm is only six years old. Mckayla thinks he doesn't understand. But he does—much more than he lets on. He breathes his mother's pain. It thumps inside his belly. He wakes up with it in his mind. When she can't sleep, he's up. When she's stressed, he has angry thoughts. *I'm a beautiful woman,* Mckayla thinks to herself. Surely, there are plenty of good men who would kill to have her. There's sure to be one who would even be willing to help raise Malcolm as his own. She has gone through a lot. But so has Shelby, Mckayla's thinking. That woman down the street has had to funnel so much on her own. Shelby has three children by the same deadbeat father. The women had once been rivals, but they have now settled their bitter feud. Mckayla was beyond astonished when she found out Shelby may not be the only wife. She learned from Shelby, Shamar was already married. Shelby is ticked off. "Not only has the scumbag evaded child support, but he has a wife in Africa," she tells McKayla. Shelby and Mckayla want to settle the score. They have been humiliated. However, "I will not stop until I find him," Shelby promises.

"*Wisdom below the earth*"

Tabitha strolls the grass field under a misty afternoon rain, looking for a little comfort. She can't erase what's happened out of her mind. It's eating at her. A measly shrug, she'd observed. Assuredly, that's all it was. Yet it keeps coming back. A prayer to her mother's corpse predicted terrible things to come. Maybe she will tell her husband. It will clear the skeptic air inside of her. Her eyes could have deceived her, perhaps. No need to allow aching in her stomach to metastasize.

Tabitha gets back to the house, her heart stiffens with unease, probing her husband.

"Shamar, sit. I have something to ask you," she guides him to a chair. "When I got robbed...uh..." her heart racing. "When we got robbed, I noticed you taking something out of your pocket, handing it to the man holding the gun to my head, as you perhaps thought I wasn't looking," she tells Shamar.

"What! What are you talking about? Have you lost your mind, Tabitha?" *How dare she?* Though he knows full well, his heart is not sincere. He has become wicked. He's running, a fugitive of the law and two brokenhearted women. His children, as well, are left to suffer. Shamar gets up, "Tabitha, dear. Whatever you think you saw must've gotten you confused," he tells her. He claims, it was the last few dollars left, emptying out his pocket. Tabitha saw him carefully wave to the armed men to leave. "Baby!" Shamar cradles Tabitha into his arms. "You're under too much stress. It has gotten you thinking and seeing some weird things," Shamar hugs his wife closer and kisses Tabitha gently on the lips.

Blue Mountain, Madagascar

Michael sips once more from the bottle, the bourbon dry on his lips. His throat burning, the more he gulps. His hands are frail yet not as brittle as his heart. Five hundred U.S. Dollars is his share of the pot. He shrugs it off as play money, gaming his hand of royal flush. All bets are off; he wins again. He wishes he hadn't.

"Are you going to bet the house this time," the man next to him jokes.

Michael doesn't even flinch. His face is rigid, afraid to hedge his hand. He'd sought counsel from the dead. One can hold a thousand secrets, but the blood of women, of children starving for truth, must never be sacrificed by a deceitful tongue. The plan has not gone unblemished. Perhaps Shamar should have escaped elsewhere—away from home, where so many hands wouldn't have to be tainted.

"All bets are off!" the gritty, huge belly fella sharing the table yells. Everyone folds, including Michael. He's lost it all. But he's free of remorse. He lets out a long sigh of relief. He's ready to go home now.

Ambanja, Madagascar

Claudine places her Cola on the ledge; the sun scouring her face through the window. "You want to know what I really think," She bows her head. "That man is crazy," Claudine picks up the cold beverage to quell the sour taste on her lips. "I mean, I'm sure there was a better way to do this," she fidgets in her seat. "Poor child, now what?" she cries to her husband.

Claudine believed it was dirty money. Shangar, however, sees it differently. Dirty money or not, it would help put food on the table.

"If you ever did that to me, Shangar," Claudine stares him down, "I would kill you."

She can't come to grips with why Shamar has gone to such a great length to deceive his wife. It is one thing for a man to hide betrayal, but to not even want to take care of his children, Claudine thinks is despicable. She also feels sympathy for Tabitha.

"It is shameful," Claudine tells her husband. She can't bear that they have allowed money to silence their souls. "Josephine once told me, whatever you take from the devil, you'll have to pay it back."

Shangar laughs and hands Claudine the unused passports.

"Such a beautiful girl. I wonder if she'll ever realize, she won't be going to America," Claudine glances at the passports. "I'm a woman. I know a woman's pain."

———

IT'S SIX IN THE MORNING and raining heavily in Nosy Be. Shamar wakes up, his eyes staring restlessly at the ceiling. He flips his head to look at Tabitha. She looks like a dove at his side. Shamar is edgy, filled with rage. The plan was for him to get kidnapped. He thought about faking his own death. He changed his mind. Seeing Tabitha again, Madagascar still had life in its blood. He could've gone anywhere. Yet he chose to be with the woman he first promised to love until death. He's contemplating his next move, but there is none. He was hoping Nosy Be would be his permanent place of refuge. A home he had come to despise. Perhaps it was guilt while he was away that made him detest home so much. Tabitha is sleeping so peacefully. Shamar traces his index finger along her back. Tabitha's body twitches. She hurdles off the bed, Startled, and feeling a cold chill.

"Why are you so jumpy?" Shamar asks.

"Just a bad dream," Tabitha tells him. Shamar's eyes look cold and wicked.

Driving to the agency to get her new passport, Shamar orders Tabitha to pull over past the traffic light. He wants to confess. Tabitha parks the car by the side of the road, ready for what she believes will be a dishonest declaration of guilt.

"Tabitha, I have something to tell you," Shamar tilts his head back and exhales a deep breath. "We're not going to America. I'm staying here with you," he tells her.

Tabitha's silence mirrors her mood. She's speechless, knowing he was hiding something. Shamar tells her, he owns gambling debts in the U.S., and there are angry men looking to make him pay. Tabitha's hands, shaky at the wheel, she doesn't know what to think or how to feel. Life seems to be crumbling right before her eyes. Looking confused, and tears falling out of her.

"Why the hell didn't you tell me this before?" Tabitha's voice searing.

Shamar claims, he had been afraid to tell her. The men who robbed them at gun point, he says, must have followed him to Nosy Be. Shamar tells Tabitha, he's afraid for his life. "Who knows what they'll do to me or even to you?" he says.

On their way back home, Tabitha's hands are sweaty. She's gasping, her foot heavy on the pedal.

"This woman called me the other day," she tells Shamar.

"Woman! What woman?"

Shamar is full of jitters. He laughs as though sobbing. The mysterious woman didn't leave her name, Tabitha tells him.

"What did she want? And what does that have to do with me?"

"She says, there's a lot I don't know about you."

Shamar's heart begins to race. He knows he has been lying to his wife. There are things Tabitha must never discover.

"Where is this woman from?" Shamar asks.

"She's coming over to the house today," Tabitha answers.

"House! Uh...Where? What house?" Shamar screeches out. He's ready to run again.

"Purple Rain"

Citadel Hospital, Nosy Be.

Tabitha is in pretty bad shape. Her body is badly battered and bruised. The doctors are trying their best to keep her alive. She was found unconscious on the side of the road, near a ravine. Luckily, a stranger recognized her and called for help. Shamar is nowhere to be found. Each time Tabitha's blood pressure drops, her life hinges more and more on a thread. She's dreaming of a good life, though her breaths are faint.

A week later, Michael rushes to the hospital. Shamar told him what he had done. Tabitha has awakened from an induced coma. The doctors worried, her brain had swelled up beyond healing. She's now stable. But not when she opens her eyes and hears an ominous voice in the room. Her blood pressure rises with every tormented breath. She's thinking to herself, they have come to finish her off. The nurses rush to her bedside.

"I think she recognizes your voice," Claudine tells Shangar.

Everyone is ordered out of the room.

"Please, let me talk to her," Claudine pleads with the nurses, refusing to leave.

They're not comfortable leaving Tabitha alone. Michael and Shangar leave the room. A nurse holds on to Tabitha's hands, as Claudine gets closer. It's a familiar voice.

"Tabitha, you might not remember who I am, but we spoke on the phone," Claudine softly says to her.

"What is this about?" a nurse asks. "The police are on their way," she warns Claudine.

Tabitha opens her eyes wider; she remembers Claudine's voice.

A month later

Michael and Shangar have surrendered. They are being held in police custody until the case is resolved. It's been a month since Tabitha nearly lost her life. She's doing much better. She's finally out of the hospital. Tabitha and Claudine sit side by side in an office at the police station. The police have allowed Claudine to recount a story that has Tabitha's heart pummeling like a death slide into hell. Shamar still can't be found. The trail of lies and wounded hearts he has left behind is far more unnerving than mysteries that had been revealed from the grave.

"Tell me, I want to know everything," Tabitha fixes her eyes on Claudine.

Claudine begins by admitting her guilt. "I'm also a woman," she says. She tells Tabitha about Shelby. How Shamar had married her as soon as he had gotten to America. Shelby made it a lot easier for Shamar to get "legal status." Shamar never told his new wife, he was already married back home. Shamar had met Shelby, who worked as a TSA agent at the airport, and was immediately smitten by her Nubian beauty. "They have three children together," Claudine tells Tabitha. What's more sickening, Claudine divulges, Shamar named his first born, a girl— Tabitha.

"I'm sure it wasn't because he missed being with me," Tabitha utters coldly.

Claudine stares at her, and lets out a few anxious breaths, unsure whether Tabitha is ready to hear more.

"Well, brace yourself, honey," Claudine reaches for Tabitha's hand.

When Shamar left Nosy Be to travel to the U.S., he had promised Tabitha, he would help find her twin sister.

"Tabitha, Shamar found her," Claudine utters each word with tenseness in her voice.

"Found who? My—" Tabitha is struggling to get the words out. She can't. She holds on to Claudine, Tabitha's body shivering, her lips wobbly, and her face stony as ice.

"Yes, sweetie. Shamar has found your twin sister," Claudine cuddles Tabitha's clammy fingers. "There is something else you should know."

Though Tabitha is no longer stone-faced, her pain is relentless under the sad look on her face.

"My sister is dead; isn't she?" Tabitha cries out, holding a stubborn mien.

"No, she's not dead. She's alive," Claudine replies.

Tabitha's heart is beating like rapid fire, faster than her thoughts can digest.

"Is it Shelby? Is Shelby my sister? I'll know it if I see her; I'll know if she's my sister. One never forgets," her lips shrinking.

"Just wait. Wait here," Claudine tells her.

The moment Mckayla walks in, Tabitha's body goes limb. Both sisters fall to the ground, crying on bended knees. Shamar had told Mckayla, Josephine and Tabitha were dead, long before the twin sisters' mother passed away.

When Tabitha took McKayla to their mother's grave, Mckayla cried a mountain of tears. "Forgive what Daddy has done. I miss you, Mama," she wept. The weight of guilt had been too much for Claudine. She found Mckayla through a mysterious voice. He called himself "Faraji." He didn't say much, only telling Claudine on the phone, "McKayla's comfort lies in Africa. There, will come soft rain." The man may have disguised his voice, Claudine nonetheless, knew immediately who it was. Weeks later, a man's body was found floating above a river, tied to a small reef. "I know that man," said a young woman who was passing by. "I saw him nearly beating a woman to death," she said. No one could explain why the river suddenly turned purple while the man lay there, lifeless.

BLACK

ROSE

BEFORE THE FALL

BLACK ROSE

BEFORE THE FALL

Yellow caution tape bordered the house when I came home. Our rented, split-level duplex in Sutphin Avenue, Queens, had turned into a house of hell. There were loud sirens and flickers of lights amidst the convoy of fire trucks and NYPD Blue. Everything was gone: Mom, Dad, our baby sister, and Uncle Jean. Nothing was left but faded memories. The only home we had ever known had burned to the ground. I couldn't let Emilio and Orlando witness such horrific sight. The next train would be pulling in the station around 4p.m. One of the detectives agreed to have an escort drive me to the train station and meet my brothers before they made it home. As soon Emilio and Orlando got off the train, seeing me standing next to a uniformed officer on the platform, they knew something terrible had happened.

At seventeen years old, a few days away from our eighteenth birthday, about to graduate from high school, this was what Emilio and I came home to. Our parents and our sister dead, our home burned down, and our only uncle with a bullet to his head. We later found out, Uncle Jean had gotten shot even before the fire started. And Orlando, well, grown men couldn't hold him down. This was how the streets had served us justice; though we had no idea what we had done wrong. Our parents were hard working people. They came to the U.S. as immigrants a long time ago. Uncle Jean had a few run-ins with the law, but nothing that would predict how gory his life would end. He loved women, taken or not. Mom always told him to be careful. Uncle Jean would laugh, telling her—roses are meant to be scattered. Still, there had to be more to the matter as to why Uncle Jean got blasted so cruelly. He would go out drinking, then get in his car, stoned. That's how he got into trouble with the law. But he didn't sell drugs. Then again, one never knows. I had friends, whose parents didn't have a clue they had turned their homes into a drug factory.

After the tragic event, Orlando wasn't doing so well. None of us were, actually. Orlando seemed to have the hardest time coping. Still a sophomore in high school, he started to cut classes regularly. It may have been because of the group home they put us into. At first, the house lady, Mrs. Ambler, didn't want all three of us in the house. Too many boys, she said. Our social worker wouldn't let them separate us. As Emilio and I would be done with school in a couple of months, our social worker found us a home a month before graduation. Emilio and I would be able to work and still go to college. The city would help us with the rent.

When we got the apartment, Orlando came to live with us. The police were at a dead-end, looking to find who murdered our family. Everyone's lips were sealed. The street wasn't talking. When it comes to these matters, not even friends talk. They're too scared. Not that we had that many friends to begin with. They will always turn on you, Uncle Jean used to tell us. It might have happened to him. Whoever shot him at point blank range, the police thought had to have known Uncle Jean. My brothers and I weren't going to fight fire with fire, not knowing how many triggers were waiting to finish us off in cold blood. So, we laid low.

When you're young, and you lose your family young, it's crippling. You have to find an escape. I took my troubles to this strip joint in Queens Village. That's where I met Jazz. She filled the void. She offered me a lap dance that nearly made me jump and do summersaults. I would go see her at least twice a week and sometimes three or four nights in a row. It was the summer after graduating from high school. I worked a security job part time at a mall in Long Island. It wasn't really filling up my pocket with much cash. Emilio also worked at the mall, selling sneakers. I didn't have money, and Jazz knew it. Still, she saddled my lap freely. There was something about her; something about us, which refused to go away.

I always wanted more, but not necessarily what Jazz thought I wanted. When   Emilio first saw her, "That's a bad chick," he hollered. I saw much more, more than her soft brown skin, and *tits* that made grown men beg to squeeze some more. She was chasing my blues away. One night, her breasts left their chocolate flavor on my lips. For sure, I thought I was going to get slapped, or beaten down by security. But Jazz's eyes locked into mine. "Little boy, don't you ever do that again," she pressed her lips against my cheek and extended a smile.

"I'm sorry; and I'm not a little boy," I kissed her on the lips.

"Please, don't do that. You have no idea what you're getting yourself into," she scoffed at me.

It was already too late. I could feel butterflies in my stomach. I was falling in love with a stripper.

The year Emilio and I enrolled at a university in Long Island was the same year Barack Obama became president. There were a lot of talks that summer about whether he was going to win. And when he did, my brothers and I were so excited. At first, Emilio and I didn't want to go to college. We then figured going to school would offer us a chance at success. But then what? America offered us a land of opportunity but then placed a ceiling over our heads. Not that my brothers and I aspired to one day run the Oval Office. "There's a reason why it's called the White House," Dad used to say to us. But when we finally had our first Black president, we were able to look up, way up, without the whip of racism affecting how far we could reach. And so, Emilio and I majored in business administration at school, thinking the sky was the limit.

I started school but still thought a lot about Jazz. I didn't go see her as much as I used to. But whenever I did, I sensed she wanted to pull away. She had once told me, her sister owns a hair salon in Brooklyn. I purposely went to cut my hair at the salon one afternoon so I could chat with Monica, Jazz's older sister. Apparently, she had been expecting me, when I inquired about Jazz. "Black," she says, "my sister is feeling you, but she can't right now." Although it was more than I expected to hear, what Monica said left a bittersweet taste on my lips. I was hell-bent in trying to figure out the air of mystery surrounding Jazz. Since Monica referred to me as "Black," I started to think, she'd mistaken me for somebody else. "My name is Romeo," I told her.

"I know," she uttered with a dizzying laughter. "It's just a woman thing," she said. "My sister likes men with your complexion."

As soon as Monica and this pretty, yellow apple skinned, thick girl started mocking me with a chant of "the darker the berry, the sweeter the juice," this tall, fair skinned Black guy with hazel green eyes walked in and went straight into a back room. It was as if a ghost had made its way in. Everyone kept quiet. Monica seemed startled, dropping the fine-tooth comb in her hand. "Romeo, if you're done, please leave," she whispered.

Taking the train back home, there was a lot on my mind. I had never met the guy who owned the salon; the one everyone seemed so afraid of. He was never at Carmelo's, the strip joint where Jazz worked. I wondered if he perhaps was Jazz's boyfriend. She told me she wasn't married. I had assumed there was no man in her life. I didn't know what to think. There was this funny looking dude standing across from me on the train. Sitting at the edge of a row of seats, I looked out the doors every time the train came to a stop. The hefty, angry looking guy would move aside to let passengers get on and off the train, and then would slide back, staring tensely into my eyes. He looked familiar, but I couldn't recall where I had seen him. He then widened his lips with an icy snicker, tapping his right hand on his thigh as the train jolted back and forth. Riding the subway every day in New York City, I could easily sense trouble. I started thinking, I was being followed. I could smell the fear in me. Especially after the guy staring at me had put his hands behind his waist. My nostrils hot, I could feel the warm air all over my lips. When the dude slid the packed holster around his waist to the front of his pants, I swore I was done. The train crowded, it didn't matter. Blood money doesn't always wait on a perfect time to cash in. At the next stop, I pushed my way past two old ladies and ran to the next train cart. The guy with the nasty grin followed me, walking slowly behind me, his hands stuck to his abdomen. Thankfully, a uniformed cop boarded the train the following station. The man following me got off. *Oh! Thank you, Lord.* Leaning against the door, my back pasted to the glass window, I breathed a sigh of relief. He had put the fear of God in me.

At the club that night, the moment I walked in, I sensed trouble. The smell of "ganja" burned heavily in the air, far more than usual. Carmelo's was jam-packed, looking as though it were hosting a "high rollers" reunion. Perhaps it was. The lines of expensive cars out in the parking lot made my head spin with envy. It was a good thing I'd brought Emilio along. It felt awful, leaving Orlando behind. But he was a knucklehead. Besides, we tried to sneak him into the club a few times with a fake ID, but security threatened to get us in trouble with the law if we ever did it again. Where Emilio and I usually sit at the club was overrun by dudes with dark shades and fancy suits. Except for that one guy sporting hair locks. He had on blue jeans, black boots, and a white T-shirt. His wrists and neck, full of diamonds. I thought, perhaps, he was a famous hip hop artist I didn't know about. Quite a few celebrities would sometimes show up at the club and throw enormous parties.

There was something else that caught my eyes. The tall, light skinned guy I had seen at the salon earlier, where Jazz's sister worked, was also at the club. He sat next to the guy with the ornamenting diamonds. He had on a white suit, with what I would bet to be a ridiculously expensive designer watch around his wrist. His shoes, no doubt, designer brand, red bottoms. "Why are you sweating those cats so much?" Emilio asked. I wasn't. I was just following Jazz's eyes—rapt into their world. She took a peek in the back, saw me waving, and yet completely ignored me. Her eyes looked lustful with greed. I didn't like the way the two flashy dudes were staring at her. I imagined them thinking about doing all kinds of things to her. Emilio noticed my wrath. He suggested for us to leave. I didn't want to. "Then let the girl do her thing," he pounded me on the chest with his fist. I was afraid to tell him what had happened earlier on the train. I didn't want to scare him. Emilio would turn into a loose cannon whenever he thought somebody was out to get us. But then, I started thinking how afraid Monica looked when the guy in the white suit walked in the salon. He didn't speak a word to anyone. Yet they all appeared to be shivering. I finally told Emilio. That's when hell erupted.

"Fuck! I can't die like this," I yelled out, running outside, and ducking behind a car.

There was gunfire everywhere. Bullets coming from heavy weapons that would have an atheist singing praises to God, or make any grown man wish he were back in his mother's womb.

121

"Squeeze the hammer at them bastards," this guy yelled out. I wet my pants.

"If only Jazz could see you now," Emilio joked. I wasn't laughing. We both waited patiently, scared stiff, until the police arrived, my heart in my throat. Finally, the parking lot was cleared. Emilio and I had dodged the flurry of bullets. I was still cringing in cold sweat—a bone chilling fear. We didn't know what happened.

It's a strange feeling, thinking somebody wants you dead, without a clue of whom it might be. I was beginning to think that way. After telling Emilio what had occurred earlier that day, he thought I was being set up. He blamed Jazz. Yet in no way I thought she was involved. Then again, the dude with a bunch of diamonds around his neck had Jazz on his lap. He was slapping her butt excessively. I couldn't take it anymore. I went to grab her. "She's my play," the dude with the Mafioso like entourage blew me off. I told him, Jazz wasn't a play toy. Out of nowhere, bullets started to fly. When the dude with the white suit slipped his hand under his jacket, Jazz told me and Emilio to run. Yet there was something even more peculiar about the whole thing. There was another group of guys in the back with their guns out, exchanging fire with the men up front. We saw Uncle Andre at the club, while Emilio and I were crawling our way out to the parking lot. Andre was not our real uncle, but since he and Uncle Jean were good friends, out of respect, we called him uncle.

Something else had gotten me riled up. When I got home, Jazz called, wanting to know if my parents were still alive. I hadn't told her anything about my family. So I lied. I told her, my parents had decided to move back to Haiti. "They must have the wrong person then," she said. It was hard for me to figure out what she was getting at. Our parents were church going people. They were never involved in any arguments with anyone, let alone take part in any criminal activities. However, Uncle Jean was no saint. I was scared to ask more questions, afraid I would discover the dreadful story behind the carnage that took place in our home. Jazz didn't want to discuss everything over the phone. She wanted to be sure of things, she said, before telling me everything she knows. She asked me to meet her at the salon in Brooklyn the next day.

Cambria Heights, New York

Orlando cut school to come with us. We didn't really have anyone else we could depend on. Emilio was reluctant to go. He wasn't sure we could trust Jazz. "I don't trust that bitch. She's just a fucking stripper," he ranted.

I wanted to fight him, but blood is blood. I chose loyalty over love.

"We Blaise brothers ride and die together," I told him. Still, there was something in Jazz's voice that reassured me, she was speaking from the heart.

When I was much younger, a lot of people used to call me "Church Boy." I was the only one who didn't fuss about going to church with our mom. I was always the quiet one. That was because Mom used to tell me to show respect and think before speaking. I had always used that word myself. And yet, when Emilio called Jazz *bitch*, it made me angry. Maybe it was because Jazz was the first girl to make my heart sing. I told Emilio, if he ever called her that again, I would cut him. "Your stripper loving bitch ass is going to get us killed," he taunted me. Stripper love crush or not, I trusted Jazz.

Emilio got all three of us guns. He claimed to have gotten them from this Panamanian guy down the block. But later admitted, Orlando purchased the Glocks from someone at school. I was in panic mode, holding a gun for the first time. I didn't like the idea of Orlando buying guns off the streets. More so than us carrying unlawful firearms, Emilio and I had just enrolled in college. We were good students. I didn't want to risk throwing our future away by us getting caught, then end up in prison. I felt worse for Orlando. He was still in high school, struggling to maintain good grades and had to deal with the mess we were in.

Brooklyn, New York

Getting off the train on Flatbush Avenue, I was scared to death. My legs felt heavy. What if I was wrong? *What if this is really a set up?* I started thinking. I had gone to bat for love—for Jazz. I was hoping my own heart wouldn't deceive me.

We got to the salon, Monica greeted me with a cold kiss. She escorted us to the back room and locked the door. The room looked like any business office. It had a desk, filing cabinets, a fax machine, and three landline phones. There were few chairs, except for a recliner behind the desk, and a single wooden chair facing it. "This looks like a raggedy ass salon," Orlando muttered. There was no one in the room but the three of us. Monica went down the steps, which had a metal door at the bottom, I assumed was the basement. Monica had told us to wait in the room. After she made her way back up the steps, she went back to the salon area and locked the door behind her. We felt trapped. Emilio was about to pull out the steel at his side; we then heard heavy footsteps.

Jazz came up with two large men; both, I gathered to be more than six feet tall, weighing no less than three hundred pounds.

"What's this? Them niggers coming to crush us?" Emilio asked.

Jazz laughed it off.

"No, just normal protocol," she said, her face stern. She wanted to know if we were carrying any weapons. When Emilio told her only he and Orlando were packing, she had them agree to a strip search and took away their guns. Emilio and Orlando weren't so thrilled with the idea. They, nonetheless, had a slight grin on their faces. But before Jazz and the two large men took us down the steps, "I know Romeo is packing heat. You lied to me. But I know you wouldn't hurt me, Black," Jazz lightly brushed her finger over my lips.

We couldn't believe what was coming out of his mouth. "Hell fucking no. Y'all niggas messing with our heads. No way! No way!" Orlando dropped to the floor, crying. Jermaine, the guy we had seen at the club with the white suit, stuck a knife into us with terrible news. We had to promise not to say a word to anyone, not even the police. Jazz was shedding tears. I didn't know what to believe—my own instinct or some shady looking guy. Yet I knew Jazz's tears were sincere. Our parents, and baby sister, along with Uncle Jean, were set up by Uncle Andre, Jermaine told us. Dre had all three of us followed, seeking more of our blood. The night gunfire erupted at the club, Dre was behind it all. He'd had his own war with Jermaine and his crew. He wanted to end it with a bloodbath that included me and Emilio.

It's hard to flee a nightmare, when it is in your blood. I didn't know what kind of operation jazz was involved with. Yet Jermaine knew too much to dismiss him as a fraud. He was helping as a favor to Jazz. He couldn't tell us everything. However, when Dre pointed me out to one of Jermaine's informants, it unraveled a trail of deceits. Dre wanted me and my brothers gone. Why? Unfulfilled vengeance. Killing our family wasn't enough. Uncle Jean took Dre's money, more than fifty grand, and wouldn't pay it back. Even so, I knew there had to be more to the story. So did Emilio. "Are you trying to tell us, the scumbag wants our family wiped out over a measly fifty thousand dollars?" Emilio asked Jermaine. We weren't getting straight answers. Whatever undercover operation Jermaine was overseeing apparently didn't involve heavy narcotics. "We don't mess with that stuff," Jermaine told us. I still couldn't understand what his operation had to do with us. Emilio had a hunch, drugs played a role with what happened to our family and conflict between Jermaine and Dre. I soon caught on. Jazz had her head down when Jermaine claimed, he and his men stayed away from drugs. Jermaine and Trey, the guy who sat next to him at the club with all the bling, had been worrying about Jazz, seeing how close she and I were getting. They had been keeping a close watch on me.

As she and her bodyguards were driving us back home, "DeAndre thinks y'all hiding dope," Jazz let out.

I started to laugh. "DeAndre! You mean, Uncle Dre?"

"Uncle? We know him by DeAndre or Dre," Jazz said.

"He was so close to our family, we called him Uncle. Stop calling this fake ass nigga, Uncle, Romeo," Emilio shouted.

"There was never any weed at our house," Orlando chimed in.

"You fool, they're talking about white powder," Emilio smacked him in the head.

Uncle Jean had been selling drugs right under our noses and stealing a good amount of the ice devil from Dre. Uncle Jean must've stored most of the missing drug somewhere else. We had a bullseye on our backs for something we knew nothing about. "If we had it, I wouldn't be taking the bus trying to see you every night," I told Jazz.

Everything seemed unreal. I wasn't myself. Hard life was beginning to change who I was. So were Emilio and Orlando. Things were never rosy, even when our parents were around. Life had completely lost its air. Betrayal changes you, even more than the pain of losing the ones you love. You can't stay the same; you become a different person. I was starting to get cynical dealing with Jazz. The Trey guy, she said, was her brother. Why had she allowed him to smack her ass? Jazz insisted that she and Trey once lived in the same foster home. Trey and his older brother, Carmelo, who owned the strip joint in Queens Village, were later adopted by their foster parents. Jazz was sent to live with another family. Trey had always been infatuated with her, she admitted. But she would always see him as her brother. Trey and Carmelo had become wealthy entrepreneurs. Their adoptive parents, both venture capitalists, passed away and left Trey and his brother loads of cash and stocks. Jazz contended, she was more a partner than an employee. A shrewd businessman, Trey tended to be impulsive—a hothead, always getting into trouble, she said. Jazz feared, he would bring her in too deep.

Though both Jazz and Jermaine swore, illicit drugs weren't part of their business affairs, I knew they were still doing shady business. Jazz owned a small share of the club, which she stated to be her sole business endeavor with Trey. Yet it was certain, she hid a lot more than she let on about their business dealings. She did blow my mind with somewhat of a mystery, disclosing, Trey was studying business at the same school Emilio and I attended. He was a smart guy but obsessed with the gangster life. Trey lived for guns, exotic cars, and women. As for Jermaine, he and I became close friends. He came from interracial parents. They disowned him, because he'd refused to give up the fast life and move with them to Germany. He and Trey had been friends since high school. Jermaine once had a terrible *coke* habit, which might have explained why he detested narcotics. "I had a habit, but I was never an addict," he would say.

Jazz and Jermaine set up a meeting for us to meet Trey at his home in Long Island. It was a long drive from our apartment on Jamaica Avenue. Jazz and Jermaine picked us up in a black, tainted windows SUV, the year's current model. I never bothered to ask, but along the miles of unending roads, I kept asking myself whether the story of Trey and his brother inheriting so much money was a ploy to hide dirty money. Orlando, Emilio, and I each brought our firearms. Even though we would have to leave our weapons in the car once we got to Trey's home. He didn't like having strangers with guns around.

We got to the house, the place was like a fortress. There were cameras lined up from the fence gate, all through the entrance pathway, and beyond. With so many eyes scrutinizing us, it felt as though we were about to be introduced to a head of state. The home was heavily guarded with men in black suits, strutting massive bulges underneath their jackets. "They're okay," Jermaine waved to a beefy guy making his way towards us.

"What's this? Are we about to meet Obama?" Orlando burst out laughing.

"I see your little brother is a jokester," Jazz said with a chuckle.

The home so massive and lavish, by no means affordable for a small-time hustler, Jermaine told us, it was an inherited estate from Trey and Carmelo's adoptive parents. Carmelo also lived there.

"Any friend of Jazz is a friend of mine," Trey yelled out, strolling down the spiraling steps. He took us to what looked like a playroom or a lounge, with pool tables, video games, large flat screen televisions, a bar, and lots of beautiful women. His brother, Carmelo, slouched on a couch, next to a chunky, caramel skinned girl with bedroom eyes. He was a big guy himself; gritty and old-school, according to Jazz, looking as though he always has the next move on his mind. "I'll be back for you," he said to the thick girl when Trey called him over to join us. We made our way past several doors, walking into what looked like a conference room.

"I feel like I'm in a mobster movie," Orlando blurted out.

We all started to laugh.

"You'll really be thinking that when DeAndre pops a bullet in you," Trey lashed out. Just that quickly, everyone's face got serious, the room quiet as a frozen chamber at a cemetery.

Trey didn't mince words. "If y'all want to stay alive, we got to take out DeAndre," he said. He spoke with shrewdness and intensity. Yet also with what I believed to be uninhibited candor.

"Y'all, I'm not sure about all of that," Emilio finally spoke.

He had been quiet, both he and Jazz. I got the impression everyone wanted me to approve the death sentence. I thought of Mom and Dad, our baby sister, Rose; how much we all had missed them.

"Just say the word, Black. We got your back," Carmelo stood up, raising both hands at his side like bird wings.

"Romeo. *Baby.* That man killed your whole family," Jazz, sitting next to me, extended her hand and cuddled my face.

Payback is a strange thing. You long for it. Its thirst is in your blood. You go to sleep, dreaming of so many ways to feed its craving. And when you wake up, your mind rejoices over its wishful delight like narcotic entering one's body. And yet, I couldn't do it. Neither could Orlando and Emilio, even though our lives depended on it.

"I know what to do. Sometimes a man is confused with too much pain to even say yes," Trey uttered forcefully.

———

THOUGH MY BROTHERS and I didn't verbally give permission to take another man's life, we knew what was about to go down. When hell rains on you, sometimes you have to blow the torch back. A week after our first meeting with Trey, both he and Jermaine paid us a visit at home.

"It's done," Trey told us. When asked how? "Don't worry, I got men for that," he answered. For the first time in a long time, I felt the emptiness of our parents and sister gone, however unrighteously fulfilled. Yet, it was being gratified with more grief. Revenge didn't feel so sweet, perhaps reflecting remorse. DeAndre was once considered family. He was our uncle. He used to boast about how much he loved us. His love was empty, however, like a hole on the ground waiting to turn flesh into dust.

"Any last words from Uncle Dre?" Emilio asked. As soon as it had left his mouth, his own words seemed to have startled him. "You know. DeAndre, I mean," Emilio muffled his words.

"If you really want to know the truth, I heard he begged for mercy like he made your other uncle plead for his life," Trey said.

Jazz joined us later on. It was time to get down to business. I didn't want Orlando in the room with us. He was still too young. He had one more year of high school left. I didn't want us to ruin his life. Orlando was already on the brink of giving up on a not so promising future after high school. College wasn't for him, he said. He had no idea what he wanted to do with his life. Losing Mom and Dad never stopped eating at him. I would sometimes see it in his eyes. He wasn't there every now and then. It seemed as though he had long made up in his heart, there would be no other exit than to leave life gun ablaze. It started with our parents' death, followed by his newfound love of firearms. And lastly, his utmost devotion to the man who helped save our lives. Trey was now like family. When a man has taken it upon himself to lift your burden of pain, he becomes more than blood relative. You owe your life to him. Trey and Jermaine became part of the brotherhood. More so, we became part of them. We were now one family. And Jazz was about to be my bride. Except, she didn't know it yet.

Trey and I bonded as though we'd long been brothers. I felt sorry for him at times. He and Carmelo came from broken homes. Both of their biological parents committed suicide. Trey was only five years old when it happened. He and Carmelo spent close to seven years in foster care, before finally being adopted. While Carmelo appeared to have moved on, Trey struggled to let go the memories of the souls that had given him birth. He remembered his mother singing to him, and his father taking him and Carmelo to the park to play. Yet he kept dreaming about empty syringes on the playground even as an adult. "You think I'm a thug, don't you?" Trey asked. I shrugged, not knowing what to say. "Outside," he said, "I'm like steel. But here," he pointed to his heart, "is full of broken glass."

Trey and Carmelo owned several barbershops and beauty salons throughout Queens and Brooklyn. Trey was taking up classes at the university in Long Island, but he was only going part time. His operation was like a street level stock exchange, without much financial incentive. Trey wasn't leveraging his wealth well enough for my taste. He was more interested in the glitter of the wealthy lifestyle and not necessarily the potential fortune his capital could further generate. The streets of Brooklyn and Queens loved him, nonetheless. As he and his crew were low interest loan sharks. Trey was like a god, lending large sums of cash to people and small businesses, which most times resulted in unresolved debts, without borrowers worrying about losing a limb or even worse. Being famous, respected, and feared in the hood, Trey relished with intoxicating thrill. He agreed to grow as an enterprise but refused to relinquish his notorious street celebrity status.

At the apex of the 2007 recession, with home values plummeting like a death ride, the market seemed primed for us. The Feds had been trying to unpack a market flooded with overvalued assets. So, we went small. Sort of like an underground street hedge fund. We bought homes and encouraged small business owners in inner-city neighborhoods to invest, promising a more than marginal return. They loved it. So did Trey. I didn't know anything about real estate, or housing development. And yet, Trey trusted me. We were going to help grow and stabilize our community, with Trey being revered even more as godlike.

Orlando, Emilio, and I moved in a modest suburban home between the borders of Queens and Long Island. Orlando was doing cartwheels because of the indoor pool. Trey paid for the house with an advance, since Emilio and I were now working for him while still going to school, full time. Jazz, as well, moved in. She had been living with her older sister Monica in Brooklyn. It didn't take much to get her to join us. Jazz and I weren't dating, nor did we ever ask each other out. She knew I loved her. I asked her to quit stripping and helped her enroll at the university. She had always wanted to study law. Thus, she chose criminology as her main course of study.

We had a lavish party at the house when Orlando was graduating from high school. Trey and his crew had the entire neighborhood shut down. He surprised Orlando with a car as a graduation gift. It was the latest model Coupe Mercedes Benz. During the party, Trey stunned everyone, proposing to Adrianna, this gorgeous blonde he'd met at school. Many of the women at the party teased him. They didn't believe he was capable of surrendering his heart to a woman for more than ten seconds, let alone a lifetime. There were a lot of men with heavy steels on their waists. What stroked me as bizarre, most of them had different gang affiliations. Among the so-called "Trey's peoples," stood Robert—a cop who also happened to be Adrianna's brother.

I understood why the street loved Trey. But one thing I couldn't shake off was—why weren't the drug dealers and other street hustlers after him? Millions of trust fund money may buy one respect and clout in the hood, but it could also bring about enemies. Trey's only gripe appeared to be with DeAndre. I found out, Dre was a small-time hustler who worked for a drug tycoon. That's when I got the answer to a clandestine operation, which changed a lot of things. There *were* drugs involved. Although not directly within our enterprise, drug money played a key role through back-channel exchanges. As "Head of operations," Jermaine was sending money across many developing countries to buy lands and build hotels. And yet, Jermaine later admitted, money was also being sent to cartels and drug kingpins to help destabilize the political climate in those countries. Profitable foreign business endeavors could only be assured with the "right people" in power, Jermaine said. While the funds were being sent to mostly third world nations with corrupt governments, I didn't like it. "Why?" I asked. Seemingly, the more chaos, the less costly the land and kickbacks to corrupt governments. Especially in certain areas. Then, the hooligans would move out, law and order reestablished, increasing market value. That kind of leverage made me sick to my stomach. We were preying on the poor. Our parents being from Haiti, they had recounted how utter lawlessness could cripple a developing nation. It stirred a spirt of repugnance in its people, against the rise of *benevolent* colonial exploits.

RISE BEFORE THE FALL

To Trey, it was like having "Monopoly" money. We weren't really scaling a legitimate profit-sharing business, other than our real estate, beauty, and entertainment ventures. There were a lot of risks attached to our housing endeavors. Almost everything was off the books. Trey wanted to pay as little as possible in taxes and maintain his street credibility. He relished spending cash on hyping up his celebrity status. I started to develop my own thirst for fame. Perhaps it was a play for power or hidden greed. I pushed for us to become more than a charitable, "run-of-the-mill" enterprise. It was intoxicating, an upsurge of adrenaline rush—as though Lucifer was pulling me in. I wanted to turn fifty into hundreds, thousands into millions, and a million into a billion. I told Trey, we needed to remove bribes to cartels from our portfolio. Only to then ridicule my own advice, as though naïve about improprieties of most corporate entities. As a small enterprise, looking to scale our brand, it was essential to establish our presence on Wall Street, turning our assets into more capital. We bought thousands of shares in blue-chip stocks and invested in high-end commercial real-estate.

My Butterfly

"Black, it was amazing what you did at school today," Jazz spun closer to me, treading with backstrokes the pool water, which started to feel like the warm sea. I blew a few kisses under her neck. Jazz's body quivered as she gasped for breaths. Her skin tasted chocolaty, her lips sweet as pecan, and her hair smelling like ocean breeze. Thinking I was imagining the aroma on her lips, Jazz reminded me, it was the ice-cream flavor we'd had earlier. Our bodies colliding like mating sea mammals, leaving us panting, it felt as though we were dancing on air. I'd already been there in my mind since our first lap dance. I had asked Jazz to marry me, abruptly interrupting a classroom lecture. The look on the professor's face was one of contemptable tolerance. "I'll do much more than that," Jazz knelt beside me after I had gotten down on my knees. "I will be the last woman you love," she said. As soon as we were done gusting bubbles in the pool, "Romeo, I meant what I said earlier. As your wife, the only way out with me will be through death," Jazz said.

Jazz and I got married at a California beach. It was a small ceremony. Emilio was the best man. He brought along, Matilda—a girl he had met at school. Monica couldn't keep it together, crying joyfully as her sister's maid of honor. Trey walked Jazz over to me, while Adrianna serenaded everyone with her lovely voice. Orlando didn't look too happy sitting next to Adrianna's brother. He thought Robert might have been an undercover cop who had gotten way too deep. Jermaine ditched the ceremony to watch over our headquarters in New York. Jazz thought there was more to his absence. She worried, Jermaine was starting to feel snubbed, my increasingly becoming Trey's right-hand man. Fearful of the violent world my brothers and I had yet come to grips with, Trey and Jermaine weren't always tolerant. Sometimes, when people couldn't pay back their loans, things happened—bad things. I couldn't really trust that things wouldn't change between me and Jermaine. Our kind of business was very much like ruthless politics: your so-called "brother" could turn around and be your worst enemy. One bad look, one word said with contempt or interpreted wrongly, could end with family burying *blood*. Trey gave me and Jazz his blessings; yet his wedding toast sounded more like a groom deserted by his bride.

The Shadow of a butterfly

Mom used to tell us about the hands on the wall when she and Dad lived in Haiti. They fluttered like wings of a black butterfly, their shadows reflecting over the wall. Rose loved hearing Mom telling those stories. She and Mom would put their hands to the light. "Look, guys. Don't they look like dead flowers," Rose would say to us. I wanted to bring back her spirit, keeping her sweet laughter alive, since we now had wings. I became Trey's foremost advisor and CEO of the enterprise, overseeing the corporation like a black king. I called a meeting, insisting we do business as The Black Rose Firm. Trey loved it. Yet, "You made me feel as if I didn't have a choice," he said with a smirk.

By the time Emilio and I graduated from college, we were both earning enough to toss our diplomas down a drain. We, nonetheless, kept a promise made to our parents. We maintained a low profile outside of work. With fast life and exotic cars, also came an avalanche of temptations. Jazz and I didn't move out of the house after we got married. She dreamed of sipping Tequila at night, out on a balcony overlooking the shore, in a multimillion-dollar home near the Hamptons. While I refused to allow her to get ensnared by our newfound wealth, it started ruling my own thirst. Jazz went to school during the day, came home, and waited for me to get home. I didn't always keep that promise. There were women everywhere around Trey. Some had husbands and children at home. It wasn't long before I joined these women in bed. Trey called our indiscretions "hotbed of lies." Adrianna didn't seem to mind. At least I thought she didn't. I never saw her complaining. Jazz seldom inquired where I had spent nights away from home. She knew the devils' glee had gotten the best of me.

Jermaine, I sensed, wanted out. He didn't appear to be thrilled with revamping of the enterprise. While we didn't technically call it a demotion, he was no longer in charge of our finances. He'd called a meeting with just the two of us. I thought, surely there would be guns drawn. Parsing each word out of me, Jermaine sensed apprehension. "Listen, Cuz," he put me at ease. "I know you've changed things. But this is still a dangerous life we live," he said. Jermaine admitted, if he had a cold heart, he

147

would've taken me out. "I ain't a real mobster," he said, laughing. He offered to watch my back at all times. But he wouldn't take sides, he said, if something were to transpire between me and Trey. We toasted to friendship and family bond. Before we parted, Jermaine left me with cryptic words of wisdom, which baffled my mind.

"You've ever played Russian roulette?" he asked. He didn't wait for an answer. "Well, that's Trey. Be careful not to cross him. He's like a loaded gun," Jermaine put his hand in his pocket, took out three bullet casings, and placed them on my desk. "He came after me once," Jermaine warned.

Life was good. There we were—me, Trey, Jermaine, Emilio, Orlando, and Jazz. All under twenty-five, young Black moguls ready to conquer the world. Carmelo wanted to stay out of the spotlight. He had gotten married and moved to the Bahamas with his wife, who had also been a stripper at the club. She made him sell the sleazy nightclub and had him cash out his share of the Black Rose Firm. She told Carmelo to stay far from what she thought was an organized crime family.

It was getting arduous as the Firm expanded to get Trey to focus on business. He so desperately wished to be a hip hop star. He and I went out to nightclubs almost every night. Engrossed in maintaining his street reputation, Trey nearly got us killed. We found ourselves in a middle of a gang war. Emilio and Orlando stayed home with Jazz. Thank God, Jermaine was with us. We had security. Yet trapped on foreign turf, I didn't know whom to trust. Most of Trey's associates at the club had different street affiliations. Heavy weapons were brought out. Jermaine shoved me aside as flying bullets narrowly took out my head. Both he and Trey took out their guns. I hid underneath a table, listening to what sounded like missiles flying overhead. I felt like a coward. It was time to get my hands dirty, finally showing Trey and Jermaine, I knew about street love and war. Nevertheless, it was more about loyalty. I held my breath, blew out a big gasp, and held it again. I then stood up, emptying out my Glock. The shells went airborne, but I couldn't hear anything. I soon realized, I was the only one holding a gun. Everyone who'd remained inside the club was on the floor, ducking for safety. The shooting war apparently had ended.

"You're a bad ass!" Trey yelled out, dipping behind a chair.

"Black isn't afraid to die for family" Jermaine pounded my chest with a fist. I must've blacked out; it took me a while to figure out where I was.

Trey wanted me to teach Adrianna everything about the business. He immersed himself more profoundly into gangster life, partying with models and spending thousands on high-priced bottles. Adrianna was disciplined. She'd led me to believe, she had what it takes to oversee the operation. Jazz and Emilio saw the devil coming. They both were foolish, I thought. But all of us were blind to who would end up wearing the devil's name.

It shouldn't have been that surprising—her eyes gazing with thirst. We had been in the office too long, perhaps. A few shots each couldn't get us that stoned. I guess we both pretended as though we were. If she'd only knew where I had already taken her body in my thoughts. I smiled with excitement. She'd lit fire in me. Adrianna couldn't have imagined heaving part of a man ever willing to offer itself.

Perhaps she did. I had no defense against her golden charm. I chased her. One touch, she began to melt like ice-cream in summer heat. "Am I wrong to do this?" I asked.

She was as willing as I had been.

"Breathe, honey. Breathe," she whispered, both of us loosening our grip of each other.

———

SLOWLY, I TURNED INTO WHAT I tussled with Trey to give up. Jermaine retreated to his own shell. His mind was troubled, not having his family around. He shared his bed with plenty of women, but I got the feeling, he wanted to settle down. He spent most of his time working from his apartment in Brooklyn. Emilio, as well, spent most of his free time indoors. He and Matilda didn't come out much at night. Jazz and Orlando mostly hung out at the house. He was like the little brother she never had. Jazz did not like to talk about her family. The hands that loved, also cut, she said. I discovered her wounds the first time we touched.

Orlando thought about going to college. He changed his mind, once again, insisting it would be a wasted effort since he was making so much money as a Black Rose associate. Robert, Adrianna's brother, increasingly established himself at the firm. He was dubbed the "enforcer," ensuring everyone kept their hands *cleaned*. He'd bailed me out of many troubles. As a cop, he had a lot of influence on the streets. Without Jermaine around, my Glock became my shield. It wouldn't take me a second to pull out. Maybe it was my way of showing Jazz, I was more than capable of fending for myself. She would relentlessly tease me about not having the heart of a gangster.

Robert seemed loyal to the badge. A well respected, and highly decorated officer, I often couldn't tell which side of the fence he called *home*. Although he hadn't done anything to dishonor the shield; I started to lose trust in him. Especially after Trey suggested for me to hand over the reins to Adrianna. He wanted her to have more control over our finances. While I understood she was soon going to be his wife, we had an impressive portfolio; our investments were doing well. Adrianna and I had jolted hips behind closed doors. She nearly persuaded me, yet again, to put my hands where it didn't belong. I stopped her. "Is that your way of planning your takeover?" I asked.

"It's okay if you don't want me. I'm *so sad*. But Trey does," she leered at me with capricious wet eyes. Then, "C'mon, Romeo. Or Black. Whatever they call you. It was just a tease. Allowing me to blow your brains out once again would be like Black-on-Black crime, wouldn't it?" she mocked, withdrawing her tears.

Things were changing for the worst, like a death spiral. A week later, Trey called me in for a meeting. It was just the two of us in the office. At first, I didn't think anything of it. But when I sat down, looking into his eyes, I knew then, Lucifer had gotten me. Sitting across Trey's desk, my transgression was staring back at me. I could feel heat inside my chest.

"How long have you known me?" Trey, playing with his gun, pointed the barrel with infrared silencer at me.

He had one eye closed, as if scoping my chest. I could hear my own heartbeat.

"For a while now," I tried to breathe gently.

Trey's eyes, bloodshot—No time to imagine. No time to even think. Jazz, Emilio, and Orlando flashed before my eyes. My heart racing, pounding without breaths. *How quickly can I pick up my Glock?* One breath, that's all it would take. One thought lost in space, before my life bid farewell.

"Put your hands where I can see them?" Trey ordered, holding his Glock with both hands.

I just about reached for my waist but thought better of it. I nervously raised my hands and placed them on his desk.

"Is it true? Did you do my woman?" Trey asked.

I decided it was best to get into his head.

"Listen, man. We're brothers. I'll do anything to stop a bitch from trying to get your ass killed."

"What do you mean?" Trey asked, looking dazed. I knew I had bought myself enough time not to get whacked in his office.

Though Adrianna said I had gotten her drunk, it was to see where her head was at, I told Trey. My confession indulged an urge to believe, both Adrianna and her brother wanted to bring us down. It helped me stay alive that Trey thought they were trying to set him up to get slayed. While I couldn't prove it, I lied about having one of our associates shadow Adrianna and Robert's every move. It bought me time, yet war between brothers loomed in the shadows as though my last heartbeat hung in my throat. Stonewalling Trey was one thing; getting Jazz to believe a lie was a different story. Every word out of me was met with a smack to the face. "I knew you would end up sleeping with her," She punched me repeatedly. I couldn't deny it; so I blamed it on having too much to drink. More importantly, however, I begged Jazz to talk to Trey. She was one of the few people he trusted. "Oh! Really! You want me to tell him to forgive my husband for fucking his fiancée," Jazz said with disgust. She was the only one I could depend on if Trey changed his mind about me. Otherwise, I would have to rally the troops and face the "Death Squad."

Somehow, Adrianna's books were short. She blamed me for the discrepancy. Thousands of dollars were unaccounted for. Trey didn't know whom to believe. He kicked Adrianna out of his house and now wanted me dead. He told Jazz, if she stayed with me, he would no longer hold any loyalty to her. He'd declared war on all of us—me and my brothers. Jermaine stayed out of the matter. He thought mindless, entangling myself with Adrianna. Emilio and Orlando scolded me with their own choice words. We barricaded ourselves in the house, terrified of what Trey would do to us. He had been paying off so many people on the street, no one could be trusted. Our friends could easily turn into foes with the right price tag. Trey once said, Orlando would be the only Blaise left unharmed if we ever betrayed him. Orlando arranged a meeting between us and Trey to settle our dispute.

We got to the meeting place—a Black Rose restaurant in East Orange, New Jersey, Orlando had been overseeing. Minutes later, a fight broke out after a heated argument between me and Trey. Guns were drawn, but no bullets were fired. I had expressed my remorse to Trey. But it wasn't enough. He wanted me to get on my knees and apologize. I refused. "Well, I'll have your bitch then," he said. I punched him in the face. We both were tussling on the floor. That's when the gun brawl nearly followed. Jermaine told everyone to stand-down, allowing me and Trey to settle the score man to man.

When we got up, Trey's nose was drenched in blood. "We're done, Romeo. Consider yourself a dead man," he hollered.

Driving home, we were stopped by a police squad car. Robert was leading the pack of men in blue. When he and his men tried to take us in, Orlando wrestled with the officers. He was arrested and later charged with assault and illegal possession of a firearm. Nothing made sense as to why we were stopped by Robert and his goons. Emilio and I were also packing heat. And yet, neither Robert, nor the other officers searched us. They did let off a chilling remark to Orlando in the police cruiser, which had me scrambling for answers. "Your brothers are left to die," the officers declared.

We called Jermaine. Once again, he couldn't help. Jazz was furious. She'd stayed home during our meeting with Trey. Returning to the house without Orlando, she wanted me and Emilio in the slammer for allowing the police to take him in. The judge didn't grant bail. Orlando was a flight risk, the DA pressed on. He told the judge, Orlando was part of an international drug ring. Our little brother ended up taking the fall for Trey's old sins. We had the funds to hire the best attorneys we could afford. But then, our wells ran dry. Trey shut down all our businesses. Most of what we owned were under Black Rose. We couldn't even afford to fight off his high-priced lawyers. Then again, we didn't want his money or anything he had ever given to us. It would have been like hedging a bet with the devil—there's always hell to pay, no matter which side of the table draws the best luck.

We couldn't fight the law with *dirty hands*. The risk of being a whistleblower, bringing down Trey and his enterprise, would also cut down good men, forced to eat from the devil's hands to help feed their families. Besides, there would be more to the war if the streets found out we snitched, albeit, it was becoming evident, Trey had violated the street's badge of honor. We knew he was in some way involved in getting Orlando arrested. Emilio and I wanted our little brother out. We were ready to fight hell to make it happen.

We found out through Jermaine, Adrianna was back in the picture. She was now in charge at Black Rose. Trey had to have known, Jermaine still kept in touch with us. When he discovered we had been pressing Jermaine to help, Trey vowed to raise hell between me and Jazz if Jermaine allowed us back in. Jermaine wanted out anyway. He told Trey, he would rather have him in a body bag than allow Jazz to be harmed. Trey threatened to fire him. But Jermaine had leverage. Pretty much the same pull Trey had on the streets. It always kept Trey on his toes. The day he purposely misfired bullets at Jermaine, anarchy ensued, nearly resulting in a bloodbath of brothers on the streets. Jermaine could not disclose much about what was happening at Black Rose. I began to wonder, how did Trey end up back on Adrianna's lap?

Black Rose Mayhem

War amongst friends

I could hear the trigger behind the bushes. Jazz thought no way that was possible. Perhaps it was all in my head. If I had been imagining things, I would've been lying in a casket. At least six shots echoed behind me. I hunkered down, then staggered to the floor, thinking it would be the day my life ends. I heard it; the tense finger tapping the steel. He fired three shots before I had a chance to run. His hand jumpy, he missed all three shots less than twelve feet away. After I had stumbled, fleeing for my life, I lay face down on the concrete outside the grocery store. *Fuck! I left the gun in the car*, I thought. As he got closer, I rolled over on my back.

"Ice?" I called out. His face edgy, his eyes flashing unease, he aimed ready to shoot, but drew back his gun.

"Run, Black. Run!" he screeched out. The war had ignited a bittersweet rage in me.

The DA offered a plea. We wouldn't budge. But then, he turned up the heat. We couldn't go anywhere without being followed. It might have been a good thing, since it had also kept Trey's lookouts off our backs. Yet Emilio and I were being harassed by the police every time we walked the streets. We had to leave our guns home. I was getting stopped and frisked, daily. The cops were like heat seeking missiles, using Emilio and I as bait to bring down the Black Rose enterprise. We got an anonymous phone call that confirmed, our cell phones were being tracked. Still, the police could've easily obtained a warrant to search the house. That got me suspicious about a lot of things. Perhaps Trey had adversaries within his camp he needed to worry about, rather than chasing me and Emilio. The police surely were hoping, Orlando, young and impulsive, would snitch. Orlando refused to talk. We wanted him out, however. And whether or not one is hostile towards the Feds, they always get their way, one way or another.

They had an informant. The Feds wouldn't tell us his name. Orlando found out it was Robert, working undercover. He had a strange code name, the guy who sneaked Robert's true identity to Orlando disclosed. "THE BROOKLYN WAY; THE BROOKLYN LOVE," was Robert's tag line. We fell for the bait when Orlando told us. We went to see Robert. He opened up, revealing information shocking my jaws open. We were left without a choice. Emilio, Jazz, and I had to cooperate.

We had reached our breaking point, which finally freed Orlando, allowing him to come home. We gave up our souls in exchange for his release. But it had a lot more to do with whom the Feds were really hunting. Black Rose had been infiltrated to entrap a bigger network of unlawful enterprises. Adrianna was a call girl, with ties to a European mob. Unbeknown to us, she'd been doing business with Trey and his men before Black Rose came to be. This was bigger than us; the Feds had bigger fishes to fry. They were using us as pawns. We couldn't tell anyone, not even Trey. How did Adrianna scheme her way back into Trey's heart? She forged hundreds of documents with my signature, in what seemingly was an attempt to show I was plotting to embezzle nearly a million dollars in cash and property. The Feds were in on the colluding initially, but then worried, Adrianna had *turned*. They began to doubt her true motives, as she insisted on keeping cover, playing the role of a devoted bride. Trey married

Adrianna. We sent an informant through Jermaine to try to break her cover; Trey got even more furious. Adrianna had already blown her own cover. "This war is about Romeo getting on top of my woman," Trey raged on.

The Feds were on the verge of moving in on another criminal network, led by a notorious drug kingpin, who, yet again, had been doing business with Black Rose through subversive commercial ventures. We weren't allowed to break our silence even then, the Feds fearful that Trey would foil the operation. I was getting the impression, they didn't really want us around after we'd spilled our guts. And indeed, the Feds started to pull away once they had apprehended their prized narcotic kingpin. Bit by bit, the Black Rose Firm was being ripped to shreds by corruption, police raids, and inside informants. It had become a shell of what used to be a flourishing enterprise. Trey headed a corporation relegated to a street enterprise. Refusing to let go of a flaming grudge, he seemed to have completely lost his wit. He shielded Adrianna as though she were in witness protection custody. He told Jermaine, he feared I was looking to take her *out*. Brothers fighting brothers, the police turned a blind eye.

No one could get through to Trey. Jermaine finally agreed to help yet just as quickly backed out. I knew it was because he was holding secrets. And so was Jazz. Trey sent her a box of black diamond jewelries. She said it was nothing more than Trey messing with my head. Without a doubt, the war was personal between me and him. I stumbled on something that had enflamed my eyes. Trey sent Jazz a text message, which read: **"Do you think it's fair for a man to taste what's mine, when I've been starving for years not to take what belongs to him? You should've been mine. Adrianna reminds me so much of you."** Jazz never said anything about receiving the text message; neither did I ever tell her I read it.

BORN
AND
RAISED

BORN AND RAISED

The Black Rose Legacy

If there's one thing I can tell you about us Haitians, we're a proud bunch. A little too resilient, *if you ask me*. Especially the men. We are as stubborn as mules. When it comes to our women, there will be hell to pay if anyone messes with them. I guess you could say, we're real men, with flaws.

My name is Giovanni Black. I was born and raised in La-vallée, Jacmel—a lush town in Haiti—about a three-hour drive from the capital of Port-au-Prince. Jacmel has always been my home. It's probably the closest thing to paradise in my view. It's been a while since I've been home. I miss family. A lot has happened the last few years, however. Things aren't what they once were. I've been living in Brooklyn for the past ten years. I had three cousins living in New York, but they're all dead. I started to laugh when my uncle told me the story. And yet, it is not at all funny. Nothing about it is amusing. As a matter of fact, it is the sort of chaotic tale that should drive someone to fall on their knees and pray to their *God*.

Who was to blame? I can't tell. But one thing I know, that's what some women will do to you. I've lost my temper a few times, all because of a woman. I don't care what any man says; there's always danger in courting women, especially when more than one is involved. It is a sure bet, the one a man's heart ultimately wants, often belongs to somebody else. And so, this is my story. More so a comical predicament to some. *I sure ain't laughing.*

Jacmel, Haiti

"I'm glad to see you."

"*Se vre*, Giovanni?"

"Of course. It's been a long time."

"I see your English is getting a lot better."

"Thanks to *you*, Rachel, *mon Amour*."

"*Oh Cheri!* Please, Giovanni. Don't do that."

"I love you, Rachel."

This is when the music stops; the strings playing inside my chest that is. This is probably the fifth time I've said it. She's yet to answer. I shouldn't care, I suppose. She knows I do. How could I not?

The girl is stunning. Her curvy hips, wavy and sleek jet-black hair, and spicy lips, I find irresistible. There are things about her that are a lot different than other girls. There are plenty of other gorgeous women, of all shades, in this part of town. Some of the girls I've met on the web chat are far more flashy. But there's always *that one*. Women tell me, I'm a fine catch. But Rachel is whom I want. I hope she doesn't think I'm only interested in her body or because she's trying to get me to come live with her in New York.

At least, that's what she's promised. I never once asked. I'm only twenty-four years old. Too young for marriage, I tell her. Rachel is two years older. She claims, she and I will soon get married. I'm not sure what that means. So many of us are trying to leave. Thankfully, I have it better than most here in Haiti. My family isn't doing too badly financially. We pretty much have many of the amenities people have overseas. Though, that's not the case for most in Haiti. It baffles me to think, a girl who wants to make us husband and wife can't even say she loves me. But of course, it's not just the words. I couldn't care less. Okay, I'll admit it. I do. But it looks as if Rachel's holding secrets. I've learned, when a woman has something buried in her heart, usually, other hearts are about to be broken. I know from having done the same thing.

Wahoo Bay Beach, Haiti

Rachel and I are back at the hotel. She's meeting with friends. I would have rather for us to spend a few more days in Jacmel. The girl has me hooked. Things are normally a lot smoother when Rachel and I are alone. I hate when Alexandria tags along. It was my second time meeting her when I picked up Rachel at the airport. I can't figure out what it is, but something about Alexandria irks me. She looks at me funny. Certainly, it could be all in my head. Still, I doubt it. When your girl's so-called "BFF" starts to eye you with a look of pity, it's not good news.

The plan was for me to take Rachel and her friends to a nightclub. I'm not really feeling it. Most dudes, I'm sure, know that feeling. When you have something heavy you want to get off your chest. It's close to the end of the day, Rachel and I are out on a stroll at the beach.

"Hey, Rachel. *Mwen renmen'w* (I love you)."

"I know, Giovanni. I know," Rachel playfully wrestles me to the ground.

"I mean, *Wale a tet mwen wi bebe. Wap fem fou.* (You've made me lose my head, baby. You're driving me crazy)."

"Gio, please. Can't we just have some fun tonight?"

"Okay. Cool. If that's how you want it."

She's pissing me off. Here I am, rolling in white sand under the cover of night with a scintillating woman who refuses to tell me how she really feels. I turn Rachel over on her back, lift her top, my head buried between her breasts.

"*Wouih*! Gio," She lets out.

Something has come over me.

"It's getting late. I think we should head back," I tell Rachel.

"Really, Gio? Don't you want me?"

"Sure. Come here," I forcefully grab hold of her.

"Not like this, Gio. Be more gentle."

"However you want it, Rachel."

She looks fixedly into my eyes, shaking her head.

'You're kidding me, Gio? What's wrong? Your mood has changed."

"Rachel," I start to laugh. "Nothing is wrong."

"Oh *mon Dieu!* (My goodness!) Giovanni!" Rachel sits up. "I have something to tell you," she rolls on top of me, rubbing my chest with her hands. "Baby, please don't get mad. I didn't

171

know how to tell you this. But I am seeing somebody in New York."

I must admit; it isn't what I was expecting to hear. Most guys wouldn't give a damn if she's already taken. We should simply have fun whenever Rachel travels to Haiti. For some reason, I do care. But—*Giovanni—you will not be a sidepiece*—not Rachel's.

"Well, aren't you going to say anything? Say something, Gio."

I stay silent, staring at her.

"Frankly, Gio. I thought you and I were going to be a fling. It turned out to be much more," says Rachel, rolling over to lie on her back. "The last thing I expected going on vacation was to fall in love. Believe me, I want to be all in on this, Gio. Give me some time to figure things out."

"Fine! When you do, let me know," I tell her.

There's something wrong with this picture. I'm lying down, watching the sunset over the coolness of a Caribbean breeze with a beautiful girl, yet it isn't enough.

Chateau Noir, Port-au-Prince, Haiti

A few of my boys and I are out at the club. They thought it was a good idea to help clear my head. The guys think it's hilarious that a stud most women tumble over could fall in love so easily. My cousin, Jeremiah, manages Chateau Noir. The club was once owned by our other cousins who lived in New York. They used to run some kind of crazy operation. My cousins, three brothers, died tragically. Jermaine, the guy who now owns the club, said it was over a girl. That's crazy. I'm too young to die over any love affair, much less a woman who isn't committed as I am. Then again, like Jermaine once told Jeremiah, love can make people do some strange things.

Kompa Lakay is playing tonight. It's Rachel's favorite Haitian band. She was supposed to join me, but we decided to give each other space. Chateau Noir is always crowded on Saturday nights. This night is special, as *Kompa Lakay* will be featured for the first time ever, with DJ Ecstasy, who has traveled from Florida. People have come from even as far as the outer suburbs of Port-au-Prince. *Oh shoot. Is Rachel here?* Alexandria is at the club. I'll go say hello.

"Bonsoir, Alexandria. Welcome to Chateau Noir."

Two of Rachel's friends from New York are with her. I don't see Rachel.

"Hi, Gio. How are you?" Alexandria, sipping on a glass of—who knows what? Greets me.

Rachel often jokes about Alexandria mixing drinks.

"Where is Rachel?" I ask.

"She's back at the hotel," Alexandria answers.

I wonder who dropped them off. This guy with a fat stomach is standing next to the girls.

"How did you get here?"

"We're here with Henry," Alexandra points to the heavyset guy.

As he and I exchange handshakes, Chantal, another friend of Rachel, is rubbing the guy's belly.

He must be the "Sugar Daddy" Rachel talked about. Chantal had met him the last time the girls were here on vacation. Personally, I think he's too old. But who am I to judge?

"Rachel told me what happened," says Alexandria as she and I are walking toward the bar area.

"What exactly did she say?"

"That you guys needed space. That's all. Don't be so paranoid."

"Moi? No way. What would you like to drink?" I ask, noticing she's done with whatever was in her cup.

"Who's your friend?" Alexandria asks. We both order Tequila on rocks.

"Who? Flex?"

"Let me get a bottle of Hennessey," Flex, one of my homeboys, shouts at the bartender. "And who's this *belle Ti Cherie* (Beautiful honey)," he asks.

"Were you asking about Flex?" I say to Alexandria.

"He's tall and cute. Priscilla will like him," she says.

It sure looks like a perfect match. Priscilla is light skinned, with pretty brown eyes. Flex goes crazy for girls who look like her. Alexandria calls Priscilla over and introduces her to Flex.

"This one is about to take some special *Gouyad* (gyration) tonight," Flex whispers in my ear.

The club is getting even more crowded. It's so packed, there isn't room to move about.

"Some of y'all are about to make babies tonight," Rico, the band's lead singer yells out.

Kompa Lakay is getting ready to perform one of the most popular songs from their latest album. Everyone is going crazy, singing along, as Rico, and the lead guitar player, hypes up the crowd with the ballad of the Haitian Kompa melody.

"Would you like to dance?" says Alexandria, screaming her lungs out to the beat.

As she and I begin to dance, her hair smelling like freshly squeezed oranges, her perfume zesty, I can't help but notice how beautiful she looks. You can tell a lot by looking into a woman's eyes. Alexandria and I are around the same age and share the same birthdays, Rachel tells me. She's an amazing dancer. Alexandria's hair, jet-black and short, a tad less silky than Rachel's. Her dark olive skin is flawless. Womanly curves fill her white cat suit. The AC must be out. It's extremely hot. Alexandria and I are both sweaty. I take out my handkerchief and wipe her face. The whole thing feels awkward. I'm feeling heat in places I shouldn't be. The Kompa melody gets even more intoxicating with each step. I feel my heart racing. I draw closer to Alexandria. I can feel her breath against mine. Our bodies are now pasted together. I don't hear a sound. Alexandria has both of her hands around my neck. I hold her waist, our hips gyrating to their own beat.

The song has gone on far too long. Our foreheads virtually glued against each other's face, I struggle to collect my breath. Alexandria's perfume is all over me. Our lips touch. This shouldn't be happening. I want her. She's the answer to my problems tonight.

"What the f—?"

Someone is tapping me on the shoulder.

CHATEAU NOIR, HAITI

CHATEAU NOIR, HAITI

The Black Rose Legacy

Whatever was going on then, I should have seen coming. Perhaps it was Haiti's lustful Caribbean air or possibly the inebriating warmth inside Chateau Noir. I nearly lost it all that night, depending on how one looks at it. It was the beginning of the eventual end no one hardly ever sees coming. It was like waging bad hands at a poker game. In the end, you're stripped naked. With Alexandria, it was her fragrance and thick thighs that got me sprung.

Chateau Noir, Port-au-Prince, Haiti

"Oh shit! Jeremiah, you scared the crap out of me."

"Relax, Gio. You look as if you've seen a ghost. Where is Rachel?"

Alexandria and I are both speechless.

"I see. Well, you guys are both adults; so, I'm going to leave you two alone. You dirty dog," Jeremiah pats me on the back as he's leaving.

"I'm sorry. Oh God, I can't believe this is happening. I must've gotten lost in the moment," says Alexandria.

"It's my fault. I'm the one who should apologize," I tell her.

"Please, Gio. Rachel cannot know about this."

"I *ain't gonna* lie. It felt good," I say to Alexandria, holding her hands.

"Please, don't do this," her voice dims.

"*Karese menaj ou* (embrace your lover)," Rico belts out over the sultry Kompa melody.

"This is bad. *M'pa kapab* (I can't)," Alexandria utters softly.

Our bodies are inches apart. I put my hands behind her waist and move her closer.

"Did anybody else see us?" Alexandria asks. Her hands are now on top of my shoulders.

"I just noticed Priscilla looking our way," I tell her.

"Oh boy. This is not good, Gio."

"What's wrong?" I ask, tears running down her face.

"Me kissing my supposedly best friend's boyfriend. That's what's wrong, Gio. This is a mess."

"C'mon now. We both know, Rachel has been playing me for a fool," I bring her an edge closer.

"Stop!" Alexandria pushes me back.

The song has finally ended. Flex is making his way toward us with Priscilla.

"Are you all right, Alexandria? It looked as if you guys needed a room," Priscilla says, making a funny face.

"Listen, I'll explain later. We have to go," Alexandria tells her.

Chase Maxwell

West Palm Beach, Florida

"Man, it's so damn hot today," Santiago tells Jermaine.

"Why don't we take a break and go back inside the house," Jermaine tosses the golf club on the damp grass.

"Hey, have you heard from Rachel and the girls?" Jermaine asks Santiago.

"Let them enjoy themselves. Haiti, I'm sure, is popping this time of the year with Summer Fest."

"Good for you, allowing your woman to go on vacation down there, alone." Jermaine chuckles. "As for me, *them* Haitian cats are too smooth to let them be around my woman."

"Those women, too, I hear. I should know, dating a Haitian woman. I swear, they can get any dude to kill for them," says Santiago.

"Don't remind me," Jermaine tells him.

"It's that sweet Haitian Voodoo magic, I guess," Santiago laughs. "Actually, I'm playing. All women have it. Spanish, Asian, White chicks, Indians. You name it. I love all women. Creole, however, is what has gotten me hooked right now."

"Anyway. If you can get your mind off women for a second, I got good news," Jermaine tells Santiago.

"All right, time for business," Santiago puts down his glass of iced tea.

"You know that club I was telling you about, I've found a buyer. He's coming from Haiti. We're meeting next week."

"Are you going to tell him about that stuff?" Santiago prompts Jermaine.

"I don't quite know yet," Jermaine answers. "He's like family. But as you know, there is no true loyalty in business."

Chateau Noir, Port-au-Prince, Haiti

I'm meeting with Jeremiah today. He's planning on purchasing the club from Jermaine. Jeremiah will be traveling next week to iron out all of the details. I don't get it. Some in the Haitian diaspora, I presume, are afraid of Haiti. Who knows? It could be because it's no longer considered home. Jeremiah says, Jermaine has been trying for a long time to sell the club. He looked for Haitian investors abroad but couldn't find any. With so many people afraid to invest or come live here, I understand their fear. But folks are starving. Who's going to take care of *home* if we're all trying to escape? The way things have been going, we need brave men and women to return home and make the first free black nation shine again. There's still life in Haiti. We're still breathing.

It made Rachel less apprehensive about meeting me, knowing that my parents are from the elite. They make decent money working in government. Which many believe is run like the mob—and notorious for stealing from the poor to enrich the wealthy, some say. But when is it ever enough? No one thinks of how to create more jobs. Jeremiah wants to build an empire here, likened to the Black Rose Firm our cousins in the U.S. used to run. Now everybody wants in. It should have been the primary goal all along. My passion for Haiti to rise is one of the things Rachel loves about me. I have a good heart, she says. I don't know anymore. There's only so much one can take. My parents have a stash of money hidden no one knows about. I'm going to hook up with Jeremiah and invest in the club. I would love to become part owner. Chateau Noir is all about glitz and glamour. We'll bring *Hollywood* to Haiti. The club is always packed on the weekends. Most nights on weekdays, it operates as a restaurant. I'll persuade Jeremiah to have us turn it into a fulltime resort if we can get more investors.

Meanwhile, I need to get my mind right. Rachel, I thought, would be the girl that finally gets me to surrender. After what happened last night, Alexandria is on my mind. I think of her hair, well-endowed hips, and thighs. But of course, Rachel is just as stunning. Alexandria has that feminine swagger. And since we're both Pisces, I can imagine how she is at other things. I couldn't stand her. Now I'm hoping she plays the part well. But what if it's a game?

185

Disloyalty

Rachel is leaving today. We spoke for a few hours. She hasn't said anything. I'm guessing, none of the girls told her about me and Alexandria. Rachel isn't yet ready to end our relationship. She said something that sort of caught me off-guard. Rachel is thinking about moving to Haiti. She's entertained the idea once. This time, she sounds serious. It isn't because of me, she says. Her parents, as well, have considered returning to Haiti. They're having a massive home built in Jacmel.

Jeremiah and I are on our way to pick up the girls to drive them to the airport. We both agree what happened between me and Alexandria might complicate things. Jeremiah thinks there isn't a woman who would forgive their man being with one of their friends.

"C'mon, Jeremiah," I laugh. "It's not like we slept together."

"It doesn't matter. The way you were all over that girl," Jeremiah bursts out laughing.

"*A monche* (C'mon man), that was all Kompa Lakay sugar," I say to him.

"She thick though. *Fanm dous* (sweet women). But you know what? You're wrong, Gio. If Rachel ever finds out, and trust me she will, you guys are done."

"She has a man. And it sure isn't me. Or did you forget?"

"I don't know. I think she's trying to be genuine. Breaking up isn't easy," Jeremiah points out.

I hear him, but I play second to no one. Rachel and I have been seeing each other close to a year. Chatting on the web was one thing. Her first time traveling to see me, she should've known my head was all screwed up. I did things to Rachel that night I hadn't done to any girl. Not even a full day after we finally met in person, I felt weak around Rachel. I'm far from that type. I've never been *in love,* if that's what this is.

We arrive at the hotel, Rachel is the first one to greet me. I don't know what falling in love is supposed to feel like. But the way my chest shivers seeing her, feels odd. The girls wait in the car with Jeremiah while I go inside to get the rest of the suitcases. Alexandria suddenly wants to tag along. She's left her necklace in the room. Halfway up the stairs.

"You don't have to worry about me telling Rachel anything," Alexandria rushes behind me.

"What about Priscilla?" I tell her.

"Trust me. I have enough dirt on her; she won't say anything. Chantal doesn't know. And oops! I've just found the necklace in my purse," she says.

As I'm getting ready to bring out the girls' luggage,

"Gio, *ou remem?* (Do you love me?) Alexandria stands in front of me, her hand touching my face.

"What the heck are you talking about?" I ask, somewhat taken by surprise.

"Did you forget about Chateau Noir already?" Alexandria runs her fingers over my lips.

I'm at a loss for words.

"Kiss me, Gio."

All I do is stare at her.

"Kiss me, Giovanni."

This time, she leans over and presses her lips against mine. It's a strange feeling. My mind is telling me one thing, my body something else. I don't want to. Her fragrance overpowers me. I feel like a coward, weak. I give in. *Damn, she's sweet.*

"Now, get the bags. I'll be back for you, soon," Alexandria pulls away from me and walks out.

At the airport, I'm beginning to wonder if something is wrong with me. Alexandria looks upset, seeing me kissing Rachel. There's no reason for me to feel remorse other than putting an end to me and Alexandria. I can't. What if Rachel ends up dumping me for her boyfriend in New York? Driving to the airport, Alexandria said something that sounded awkward. She asked if Rachel was going to call off the wedding. My stomach twisted at the thought. The car quiet enough to hear Rachel groaning in the backseat of the van, I was dying to ask which one of us Rachel is planning on dumping—me or the guy she was returning to. Alexandra quickly added it was a joke. But she has been talking a lot (one of those friends) without saying much.

There seems to be more going on than the girls are letting on. I found out, Chantal is married. And that guy Henry isn't the only guy she's seeing in Haiti. I thought the girls were again joking around, until the other guy showed up at the airport with a bouquet of roses. He'd also met Chantal through a social network site. Having lived in Haiti all my life, everything about him tells me he's from money. Jeremiah recognizes him. Tito, Chantal calls him, owns several retail chains throughout Haiti. Things are getting more unsettling by the minute. Tito and this chubby looking dude are traveling with the girls. On their way to the check-in gate, "Santiago will be coming along with Rachel next time," Alexandria whispers in my ear, kissing me farewell. *Odd.* A week ago, Jeremiah said a guy name Santiago will be coming to Haiti in July to talk business. That's the same months Rachel will return. Something smells *funny.*

AUTHOR'S NOTE

Shai's Paradise, ***Black Rose, Born and Raised, and Chateau Noir, Haiti,*** were previously published as e-Books

Alexandria's Web, will soon be released as part of the *Black Rose Legacy series*

Thank you for your purchase

Follow Chase Maxwell on Instagram

@Iamchasemaxwell